NINIAN FIRE
DOUBLE DUTCHMAN

Kate Anders

First published 2011
by ElcaMedia Publishing BV
Siriusdreef 17-27, 2132 WT Hoofddorp, The Netherlands

Printed and bound by Crowes, Norwich, United Kingdom

ISBN 9789081653114

This publication has been produced to minimise its environmental impact, conforming with ISO 9001 and ISO 14001 standards, using vegetable based inks and FSC certified paper.

This novel is a work of fiction. The names, characters and incidents portrayed in it are the work of the author's imagination. Any resemblance to actual persons or events is entirely coincidental.

Cover design by ElcaMedia BV

1

Wie ben ik? *(Dutch)*

wie – who

ben – am

ik – I

My name's Ninian Fire and I set up Ignis Investigators. I'm crazy about codes and languages so I'll probably go and train to be a spy when I leave school.

On my bedroom wall I've got a portrait of myself. It's a pencil sketch really, done by Tabi, and she went over it in watercolour later. It was part of some training Dad had done with us a couple of summers ago. He'd said that if we could draw people carefully it would teach us to pay attention to detail. It was supposed to make us more observant. Tabi's really good at drawing and I was so pleased with the result that I stuck it on the wall when she gave it to me. I won't go into details about the one I did of her. She put it in the bin so it'll have been recycled by now. It's probably been turned into a paper cup or something.

In the drawing you can see I've got rather a long face, with a long nose to go with it. My mouth's straight so Dad says I look as though I don't smile a lot, though that's not true. I've got black hair and it usually flops over my face a bit at the front; Tabi wouldn't let me move at all when she was drawing me so she could get that in properly. She said it was something to do with angles. My face is quite pale. I've got greenish eyes. The only distinguishing mark I've got is a scar on the palm of my left hand, from putting it through a pane of glass when I was three. I remember that day well because it hurt like mad. But of course you can't see that in Tabi's picture because it's only a portrait.

When I was small my father was being moved round a lot, by the government I think, so I'd lived in three countries by the time I was ten. I know some people wouldn't like that; some of my mates at school have said they'd hate changing schools. It's never bothered me. Anyway I'm still in contact with quite a few friends from those days, in the Netherlands for example, and I even meet up with some of them occasionally. I've always gone to international schools and a lot of people there are used to that kind of life. It doesn't really make me any different.

Because of all the moving round I speak quite a few languages. I'm really fluent in Dutch and pretty good at French, for example, and know quite a lot of other words and phrases. I picked up Dutch and French just by being in the right place at the right time, which makes things really easy. It's the way to pick languages up without having to think about learning them. And once you realise languages are like codes it's such fun to be able to use them.

Mum and Dad run a language school in the centre of Norwich. I guess they got tired of moving round different countries. I haven't got any brothers or sisters but I chill out a lot with Tabitha and Miles, my cousins. Tabi and I are nearly the same age; I'm just a few months older than her. Miles is quite a bit younger but he's really cool. Sometimes people think we're all brothers and sisters together because Tabi and Miles and I look kind of similar. It's not really that surprising, I suppose, because my father and their father are identical twins.

Tabi's and Miles' mum, my aunt Julia, runs a catering service. I never do the 'aunt' thing actually when I'm speaking to her.

Julia is an awesome cook. She provides the most amazing food for weddings and funerals and parties. As you can imagine I'm round there rather a lot when I get the chance. And sometimes I'm helping mum at the Phoenix School of Languages, which is our language school. Our surname is Fire, so Phoenix... get it? I just love words, and where they come from.

Phoenix: *Also known as firebird. A legendary Arabian bird, worshipped in ancient Egypt. It burned itself every 500 years and rose up again from its ashes.*

Dad still disappears abroad from time to time, supposedly recruiting students to come to Norwich for language courses with us at Phoenix. I'm quite sure that's a cover story, though, because several things have convinced me that really he's a spy.

2

Pawn: a small chess piece of lowest rank
Pawn: a manipulated person

Do you attend the boring kind of school, the kind where you waste half the day moving aimlessly from classroom to classroom, or waiting for ten minutes at the beginning of each lesson while everyone gets their books out, or falling asleep while the teacher says the same thing five times?

If so, you'll just have to cross off the days on a calendar until you can leave. I'm really lucky because I go to an international school in Norwich that's nearly always fun. There are people here from all over the world. The teachers actually care about the pupils. The lessons are in English but for most subjects the teachers give you a list of work to do and a deadline. It's up to you when you do the stuff before the deadline. You go and find the teachers to help you when you're stuck. Everyone speaks at least two other languages so we know a lot about the rest of the world and not just the tiny dot on the map where Norwich is. Not that Norwich isn't a cool place to be.

The school's called Flame International School, Norwich, so it's that fire connection again. That's because the school's run by Tabi's and Miles' dad, my uncle Paul. He's the head teacher.

On the last day of school before the Easter holiday I was playing chess with Jasper, who's from Canada and is completely hooked on chess and computer games. He doesn't just play the computer games; he invents them. I'm beginning to wonder if he'll turn into a computer himself one day.

'Rather strange sandwiches today,' Jasper commented, moving his knight unexpectedly and showing me I'd completely forgotten to defend my queen.

'That's because Mrs Harwood's already gone to Spain,' I told him.

Mrs Harwood is the kitchen manager at school who always makes seriously delicious sandwiches and salads for our lunches. She's Spanish and has all sorts of recipes she tries out on us. They are almost as good as the things that Julia makes.

'Apparently they had the sixth years doing the sandwiches at break. I bet half of them have never made sandwiches in their life,' I added.

Jasper flapped open his sandwich and looked inside. 'I hope they washed their hands first,' he said darkly. Oh, gross, I thought, visualising Paul van de Berg's fingernails; he's a guy in the sixth year who is really into bike maintenance and even smells of oil. And I don't think he's ever heard of soap.

'Are you off anywhere in the holidays?' Jasper continued, as he removed my queen from the board and did something surprising with one of his rooks.

I moved forward a pawn, making sure he couldn't take it, and he swept unexpectedly across the board with a bishop. Sometimes I think he distracts me on purpose. He always wins.

'Nope,' I said. 'I guess I'll be helping out a bit at the language school.' That's always good for pocket money – straightening chairs after lessons, cleaning the board, sorting course books and stuff like that. Mum's quite generous when I help. 'What about you?'

'Working on Crossfire Nought 7,' he said at once. Jasper's been working on Crossfire Nought 7 for ages and from what he says it'll be a really cool game, when he's finished inventing it that is.

I finished the piece of ham, at least I hoped that's what it was, that had fallen out of my sandwich, and shifted another pawn, thinking perhaps I could then move a rook without him noticing that it would place his queen in trouble on the other side of the board.

I'm not sure where he'd been hiding it, but Jasper moved another bishop forward and took the pawn.

'Check,' he said. 'No, checkmate. Sorry,' he added, a bit casually I thought. I know I'm not much good but I reckon playing with him ought to teach me something. Only maybe it's not such a good plan. I don't seem to improve at all.

I felt a bit like a pawn myself, as if Jasper had known from the start I was going to lose and had just been manipulating me.

I didn't realise that I'd feel even more like a pawn very soon indeed – while observing criminal activities!

3

Surveillance: *a vigilant supervision; spy-like watching*
Ignis: *Latin word for fire*

'Yes, the new group arrives tomorrow,' Mum was saying into the telephone. 'Fifteen of them, and staying for two weeks; we'll test them on the first day as usual.'

I spread some margarine on my toast and reached for the lemon curd. It was a good feeling that the holiday had just started.

We get new groups of people coming for English nearly every week throughout the year. They don't usually know each other when they arrive. They stay at local hotels and come to our language school for lessons. It's easy for Mum and Dad because we live in a flat above Phoenix, which is quite a big building, so all the teaching goes on downstairs and in the basement. We're in the centre of Norwich and the students like that as they can visit the castle and hit the shops for souvenirs and things. They love going to the Broads for boat trips at the weekend too.

Most of the students who come are adults and they come in all ages and sizes. Sometimes they have only just left school themselves. I don't usually have much to do with them but there are some friendly ones sometimes who ask me about Norwich and its history and things. They're desperate to practise their English and it's fun hearing their accents and guessing where they're from. They never seem to have heard the name Ninian before, either. Actually it's also fun hearing what they say to each other in their own languages. Because I speak quite a few languages myself I can often follow their conversations when they're talking among themselves, and you wouldn't believe some of the things they talk about. Sometimes what they say is really weird! In the evenings Mum and Dad run courses in all sorts of foreign languages, like Arabic and Dutch and Hindi, all year round. Tabi and I are allowed to join in sometimes if Mum gets worried the groups look too small.

Mum had finished chatting and started clearing the table.

'I might need you to help tidying the classrooms this week, Ninian,' she said. 'We've got a lot of students in and I'd be glad if you could do the usual – chairs, tables, board and the bins?'

'Sure,' I said. 'Um – usual rate, right?'

She smiled. 'No problem,' she said. 'I'm assuming you'll be seeing Tabi and Miles today?'

'Guess so,' I replied.

I'd already planned to text Tabi that morning. One of the things I like about school holidays is hanging round at Tabi and Miles' place eating Julia's cooking. It's unbeatable. Monsieur Lesage, my French teacher at school, has told us about this famous writer called Proust who said that every time he tasted a madeleine cake lots of long-lost memories came flooding back to him. I'm sure every time I taste chocolate cake when I'm old I'll think of Tabi and Miles' kitchen.

'Dad's back at the weekend, isn't he?' I asked Mum.

'Yes, that's right,' she said. 'He's hoping to arrive at Norwich airport on the Saturday afternoon flight. He plans to stop over in Singapore on the way back.'

Dad had been in China, on a business trip for the language school. There are foreign businesses and universities who send people on courses with us.

'Is it really business this time?' I asked. I was sure that lots of

Dad's business trips weren't really what they seemed. Last year he was in Norway for four days 'on business' and as soon as he was back it was in all the papers and on television that a huge drug ring had been rounded up.

'Never you mind,' she said, drying her hands. 'I'm off downstairs. Help yourself to anything in the fridge and I'll see you this evening.'

Ignis Investigators consists of me, Tabi and sometimes Miles. Tabi and I are quite a bit older than Miles but he's pretty cool. Every holiday we carry out various investigations and practise codes. Sometimes we text code messages to each other one day, and it's like a competition because we have to have broken the code by the next day. Then we give each other prizes, which are usually pretty stupid ones. Tabi makes things with beads, like little bracelets. I don't wear them but I do save them in a drawer. She is good at making things like that. Miles likes liquorice bootlaces so that's what I usually give him.

Dad says that with the languages I speak and being observant I should be invaluable in all sorts of jobs when I'm older. He also says we'd make a good team. I wonder if I was cover for him or something when we were living abroad and I was little. That's if he is a spy. I mean, you wouldn't expect James Bond to have a wife and baby with him, would you?

* * *

'Surveillance game, right?' said Miles, swinging his legs off the garden table and going over to check the frogs in the pond. We were in my garden, which is at the back of Phoenix. Julia had shovelled us out of her kitchen as she'd had a big order for a party and said she didn't want us under her feet. Tabi and I looked at each other. 'Sounds good,' we said in unison. I'd still got my feet on the table.

9

Tabi waved a hand in the direction of them. 'Your trainers are wearing out,' she said critically. 'The soles are all cracked and I think there's a hole.' I didn't reply. They were really comfortable and I wasn't planning to waste holiday time in shoe shops. I made a mental note not to let Mum get a good look at them.

'Can I pick the first name?' asked Miles. He swished the pond water with his fingers and straightened up.

'Names in a hat,' I said. 'It's the only fair way.'

We've done that before. We choose one of the Phoenix students from the lists of names that Mum puts up in the entrance hall and shadow them for a couple of days. We take it in turns to choose someone. It's great practice for us and usually surprisingly interesting. Last holidays there was a really gross lady from South America called Dolores something-or-other who told everyone she was writing a book about Norwich Castle, and in fact all she did was sit in cafés eating cakes. Tabi had chosen her to follow. Dolores never even visited the castle once and it's worth seeing. You could spend a whole day in there even if you didn't like history.

We went in to the entrance hall of the language school. I knew Mum would be in her own office along the corridor. Sharon is the Phoenix secretary and on weekdays she's always at her desk at the entrance to Phoenix so that she can welcome students and tell them what lessons to go to and things like that. She wasn't at her desk now as it was Sunday.

'We need someone who arrives this week,' I said. 'Let's look at the new list. It must be around somewhere, because they're starting tomorrow.'

'Here it is,' said Tabi. She'd found the A4 size sheet pinned on a notice board next to Sharon's desk. Passport sized photographs were next to each name. This makes it easier for us when we're planning to follow people, because we know straight away what they look like, but Sharon puts them up so the students get to know each other quickly and so the tutors know who everyone is.

'Quite a few Dutch ones, a few French – oh, and a couple from Japan...' Tabi was running her eye down the list.

'Let's have a look,' said Miles. He looked up at the list. 'Ferdinand Rameau from France – no, Switzerland. Maybe... oh here's a good one. Thor Rasmussen from Denmark. We've just been doing Norse gods at school and Thor's one of them. I choose him.'

'OK,' I said. 'I'll have Ferdinand Rameau.' I like Switzerland and I thought 'Ferdinand' sounded rather good. 'What about you, Tabi?' I asked.

'I'm having Nikita Mizuno from Japan,' she said. 'I like her hair.'

I didn't think there was anything special about her hair, but Tabi's like that sometimes. When she gets together with her friend Chloë all they think about is doing each other's hair.

Tabi took a sheet of paper from the reception desk and wrote the three names carefully on it. Then she tore the paper into strips, each with its name, and folded them up.

'This'll do,' said Miles, picking up the waste paper basket, which was empty. Tabi put the three pieces of paper in it and shook the basket a little to mix them up.

'Off you go, Miles,' she said. He reached forward with one arm inside the basket, looking away so he couldn't see which paper he took. Then he unfolded the paper.

'Yes!' he shouted, then realised he needed to keep his voice down. Mum might hear us in her office and wouldn't be pleased if we were hanging around Phoenix. We certainly didn't want her knowing we were planning to follow students round Norwich. 'My choice! Thor Rasmussen!'

I looked round and glanced through the glazed front door, down the steps to the street. This was going to be a good start to the holiday, even though it wouldn't be Ferdinand we'd be following.

'We'll need his address,' I said. Tabi moved to where Sharon would usually be sitting at the reception desk. 'There's another list here. Rasmussen. Got it! He's staying at a hotel in Earlham Road.'

Miles and I looked at the list she'd found and we quickly memorised which hotel it was. Miles was checking the notice board again. 'He's only signed up for mornings, for two weeks,' he said. 'So that leaves us every afternoon to follow him. Cool!'

I didn't want Mum coming to find out what we were doing. I led the way down the steps onto the pavement.

'His hotel's easy for us to get to,' said Miles, as he wrote Thor's details importantly in his black notebook. It's one of those useful notebooks that has a loop on one side to take a pencil.

'Yes,' said Tabi. 'Remember when that German guy was staying all the way up Newmarket Road by the roundabout, at that bed and breakfast place, and we had to hide in the next-door garden?'

'Oh, don't,' I said, groaning. 'And that woman came out with her spaniels and let them off the lead, and they went straight to where we'd been hiding in the bushes.'

Somehow I didn't think Mum and Dad would have liked to hear what the woman with the spaniels had said. It had also made it worse that the German had come out at that point and had had a perfect view of us being chased off the next door premises. He'd been able to see us so clearly that that had been the end of the surveillance exercise. So we'd never found out what he'd got up to on the rest of his Norwich visit, apart from going to his English course, that is.

I knew Thor would be arriving at a quarter to nine the next morning for his English test and first lesson. We'd be outside his hotel before that to accompany him to Phoenix without him seeing us, and we'd be waiting for him at twelve o'clock when he came out.

I wondered how he'd be spending his afternoons. We'd have fun following him and finding out where he went.

'D'you want to see my new bike, Ninian?' asked Miles.

'Sure,' I said. Miles had just had his birthday and I hadn't seen his main present yet. He'd been waiting for that bike for months. 'Shall we all go down to the river?' I suggested. Behind Miles and Tabi's house there's a park which is good for biking, and if you go through the park and out the other side and down a bit you can bike for ages along the River Wensum.

I ran back up the steps of Phoenix and into the flat. I grabbed my cycle helmet, iPod and bike key and shot down again. My bike's always kept in the back garden, under a tarpaulin. I opened the side gate and fetched it.

'See you at your place!' I shouted, leaping onto it. It'd be easy for me to get there before they arrived to pick up their bikes, even if they ran. An afternoon by the river, and then we knew what we'd be doing for the next few afternoons.

Or so I thought.

4

Cryptography: *the practice and study of hiding information*
Code: *method of obscuring a message*

It was nearly supper time. I put my bike round the back, locked it and went up the steps to Phoenix, and then upstairs to the flat.

We'd spent the afternoon by the river as planned. Miles' bike was silver and dark blue, with seven gears, and a bit big for him, but looked really cool and I guess altogether he'd biked much further today than Tabi and I had, looping in circles round us and going on ahead. He'd let me have a go on it too although I'm too big for it, and it had been a good feeling to ride a new bike. Mine's second-hand and could do with some maintenance. Maybe I'd start dropping some hints in the direction of Mum and Dad nearer the summer. My birthday's in August. When we'd got back to their house we'd found Julia had put some of her most special chocolate cake out for us, which hadn't take us long to eat. I hoped she'd meant us to finish it.

Mum heard me coming in and called along the hall from the kitchen.

'Ninian, Dad called. He says he's sent you an important email. And he sends his love.'

'OK Mum, thanks,' I called back. I switched on my computer and while it warmed up I put my bike key and iPod on my desk and flung my jacket and cycle helmet on the bed.

Two emails had come in. One was from Jasper, the guy I play

chess with at school; he'd sent me a couple of links to the game he was working on. I'd look at that later. Dad's email was marked priority. What was he sending me? I'd be seeing him again in a few days. I was looking forward to fetching him with Mum from Norwich airport. Dad always flies in via Amsterdam; there are four flights a day to Norwich from there.

As I clicked Dad's message open I saw it was completely in code.

Dad started giving me coded messages for fun when I was quite little. He taught me that there were all sorts of different kinds of codes, and how to work out what kind of code a message is in.

'Ninian,' he told me. 'I know you realise how important languages are, and codes are like languages. They're just a different way of saying things.'

I'd then been given a long lecture about how learning languages makes you think logically and in patterns, so your brain gets trained to work all kinds of things out efficiently. Apparently people who speak several languages have brains that look different from those of people who don't. Not that I fancy anyone looking at my brain. Later Dad told me that nowadays there are computer programs to design and crack codes but even so some still have to be worked out by people instead.

The first line of Dad's email read: 19 9 14 7 9 18 15 6 5 7 1 19 19 5 13. Would I be able to decipher it? I knew Dad would expect me to spend as much time as it took to work it out and he'd be really disappointed if I couldn't crack it. There was a much longer message underneath and my heart sank as I looked at it. It looked like this:

YYCOOJUN
JGCLBWPR
1045

UCAYXSYF

THZIAOLH

GLTMLZXONK

Wow. I pressed 'print'.

'Supper's ready,' called Mum from the kitchen.

'Coming,' I called back.

I tucked the printed message carefully under my pillow. After supper I'd start with the number code as it was shorter. Dad would be home in a few days anyway so I wondered what he was telling me now that was so important. Or was he asking me to do something for him?

At supper I told Mum about Miles' new bike and that we'd been down by the river that afternoon.

'Did you find Dad's message alright?' she asked.

'Yup,' I said.

Mum had told me she was going to something at the Theatre Royal that evening with a couple of friends from her book group. As soon as I was back in my room after supper I got out the coded message from under my pillow and looked at it carefully.

There are all sorts of special expressions you can use when you're talking about codes. For example, the original message that you're actually sending someone is called 'plaintext' and the message once it's in code is called the 'codetext'. So if you said 'attack the castle' that would be plaintext, but if you said 'the sun's bright today' that could be codetext if the person getting the message knew to attack the castle if they heard the word 'bright' in any message at all. If you see what I mean.

The really difficult codes to crack are the 'idiot' codes. They're nothing to do with being stupid; they're the ones created specially by the people using them, instead of well-known code patterns. And now you can get all kinds of computer programs to crack codes, idiot codes are the safest.

A few years ago at school we did codes in maths. The easiest one was A=1, B=2 and so on, all the way through the alphabet. So as long as you know what order the letters are in the alphabet, it's easy to work out what the message is. You can put the message in other alphabets too, like Greek for example. That's very useful if you're trying to make it hard for people. Tabi sent me a coded message in Greek once.

I looked at Dad's number message again, hoping it was the easiest kind because the letter one was sure to be more difficult.

19 9 14 7 9 18 15 6 5 7 1 19 19 5 13

Quickly I took a pad of paper and a pencil from by the computer and, lying on my bed, copied the numbers. Then I wrote the alphabet out and numbered each letter from one to twenty-six.

I pencilled each corresponding letter under Dad's numbers, and it came up like this:

S I N G I R O F E G A S S E M

'Sing...' I could see the word 'gas' clearly in the middle but the rest didn't make sense. Perhaps the letters were numbered differently. That's one way to disguise a simple system. So instead of A = 1, you can make A = 2, B = 3, and so on. I tried that.

R – H – M. No, that wasn't going to work. How about the alphabet backwards? When Z = 1, and Y = 2? H – R – M. But as I looked at Dad's message more carefully, I saw that all he'd done was use an old trick. He'd used the basic number code of A = 1, and just written everything backwards! I could read it easily now.

M – E – S – S – A – G – E – F – O – R – I – G – N – I – S

Message for Ignis! I'd got the plaintext.

Dad knew I'd started Ignis and that we liked sending each other messages, and that we did a bit of surveillance practice from time to time. I hadn't actually told him that we followed students from Phoenix. He had warned me once not to get Miles too involved as he was younger. Miles does occasionally have nightmares if he's been watching a scary movie or reading something that sends shivers down your spine. Dad told me that as I was the oldest I had to take responsibility for 'making the right judgments'. I guess he'd decided Tabi was capable of looking after herself. She definitely is. And really I reckon that Miles is pretty tough.

Well, I was glad neither Tabi nor Miles was here, in case they'd have spotted Dad's trick before I had.

Now there was the question of the letter code. It looked a lot harder and I guessed it almost certainly was. Dad had wanted to make sure I'd decipher the first one easily but I knew he liked making me work at things. This could take a long time. Should I get Tabi to help? Would she be fed up if she thought I'd left her out and managed to crack it all myself?

The letters didn't look as though they were in any particular language. There were far too many consonants for that. I wondered if some of the letters were used randomly, in other words just put there in no particular order, between the letters that mattered. But the message wasn't really that long so probably every letter was needed. And anyway there were the numbers. Perhaps they weren't in code at all. What's more, some of the letters might be Roman numerals.

After trying quite a few ideas out I knew I had to give up and wait till tomorrow when Tabi would be here too. Maybe if we put our heads together we'd be able to work it out. Dad was going to be back this week and I didn't want to have to face telling him I didn't know what he'd sent me. That would be really embarrassing.

For a while I did some stuff on the computer, including checking out Jasper's links. His game looked as though it was coming on really well. I'm sure Jasper will end up a millionaire once his games are in the shops.

But I did wonder what Dad had said, and what it was that he wanted Ignis to do.

5

$$3 - 1 - 19 - 3 - 1 - 4 - 5$$

I'd sent Tabi a text late in the evening and she'd promised to come round straight away the next morning. I was sitting on the flat stairs waiting for her and finishing a piece of toast and strawberry jam when I heard the side gate slam. She must have cycled over.

'Miles can't come,' she told me, pulling off her cycle helmet as she came up the stairs into the flat. 'He's been invited to stay at his friend Colin's. He says he's sorry and we can carry on without him but can we save Thor till he's back... but of course we've got this to do now. Wow, Ninian, your room's a mess,' she added as she came into my bedroom.

'Yea, well, I know. I'll tidy it at some point,' I said. I had to admit there were rather a lot of heaps of junk lying around, including some old games I haven't played for a long time, and quite a few clothes, and some old magazines and even piano music from ages ago. I'd get round to all that eventually.

I'd printed a copy of the message for her, and we each looked at our pieces of paper.

'At least the first part is easy,' Tabi smiled. 'Pity the rest isn't like it!'

I didn't mention I'd been stuck at first. After all I should have been able to work it out without even using pen and paper.

'I've tried some basic things, like reading every other letter,' I said. 'But there aren't enough vowels as far as I can see.'

'At least it's not a different alphabet,' Tabi pointed out. 'But why didn't your Dad just write the whole message in the first code?'

'He'd never do that,' I said. 'It would be too easy – he always makes me work. But I really don't think he's sent me anything quite like this before.'

'If only there was a number at the beginning, we'd know how many letters to count to find the ones we need,' said Tabi.

Some codes need a book to go with them. So if they say '51' at the beginning, for example, you know to take page 51 of a book you've agreed will be the key. It can be any sort of book as long as there are enough words on each page. It could be a detective story or something. Then if the code says '2 – 88 – 44' you take the second word, and the eighty-eighth word, and the forty-fourth word, and so on, and make up your message like that.

'I know, that must be it!' I exclaimed. 'The first message must have a clue in it that tells us how to read the second one!'

'Sounds good,' said Tabi. I stared at both messages again, and at the letters I'd pencilled in to read the first one.

'Ignis,' I muttered. 'Ignis... that has to be it. Dad knows about Ignis but he doesn't usually mention it. It's some kind of idiot code.'

'There are five letters in Ignis,' commented Tabi. 'But that's no use here.' She was right. If you wrote down every fifth letter of the coded message, O – G – P and so on didn't mean anything, and starting from the end of the message L – H – Z couldn't be right either.

Then I thought of something. Dad had used a number code to start with, so perhaps we needed to keep using it.

Ignis in the basic number code he'd used was 19 9 14 7 9. That was it, wasn't it? Maybe that was the pattern we needed.

'Hang on, Tabi, I think I've got it!' I exclaimed. 'We use the numbers of Ignis, again and again, through the message! The nineteenth letter is... A... and then... No, forget it.' I felt really disappointed. We HAD to crack it!

'That's a great idea and it has to be right,' said Tabi rather seriously. 'I mean, why would Uncle Leon just do one short message first if it wasn't to help us with the second part? After all, he does actually want us to be able to read it in the end. And Ninian, the first message is backwards, remember.'

Then I saw how stupid I'd been; Dad's message was backwards to confuse me but he'd used an ordinary alphabet code. 'Ignis' must have been mentioned as the key. I wrote 9 7 14 9 19 at the bottom of my page, rather large, and traced over them with my pen as I thought. I just had to crack this. It was something to do with those numbers. I thought about the alphabet. And I remembered another code that Dad had used on my birthday card last year.

'Wait!' I shrieked. Mum looked through the doorway.

'Are you two alright?' she asked.

'We're fine, thanks,' answered Tabi. 'Just working something out.'

'You're round here early today, Tabi,' Mum continued. 'I'm off downstairs before all the new students arrive. Do help yourselves to anything you want in the kitchen. There are some biscuits in the box by the sink.'

'Thank you,' said Tabi. I grunted thanks, but I was busy writing. Tabi came to look over my shoulder.

'Got it, got it, got it!' I said proudly to her. Thank goodness we were going to be able to read it after all. It would have been awful if I'd had to tell Dad we hadn't been able to work out his message.

'Look,' I said. 'You were right, Dad did put the short message first so we'd use "Ignis" as the key word. It isn't every ninth letter, and then every seventh letter, and then every fourteenth letter, and so on. It's nine letters after the real one. And seven after the real one.

And fourteen after the real one. And so on. So all we do is count back. It says Y first, so count back nine letters from that and you get P. The next letter is Y again, but the second letter of Ignis is G which is number 7 in the alphabet, so just count back seven letters from Y and you get R. D'you see? And of course the alphabet goes round in a circle anyway, so after Z comes A again.'

If I hadn't been able to speak Dutch I wouldn't have realised so quickly that Dad's message started with someone's name. Names can be really confusing. We counted on through the rest of the message together, so we wouldn't make any mistakes, writing down as we went. Fourteen letters back and write it down. Nine letters back and write it down. Again and again we used the pattern of 9, 7, 14, 9 and 19. By the time we'd got to the end we'd got this:

PROFVANZANTENNWI1045NORFOLKWAYSURVCASCADELOVED

'It's strange really,' pondered Tabi. 'Those numbers in the middle, I mean...'

'Yes,' I agreed. 'It can't be a phone number. Anyway, let's write it out as words now.'

'New piece of paper,' said Tabi, reaching for my notepad that I keep on my desk and tearing off a sheet. She was pressing on my atlas, which is always out somewhere in my room. I look at my atlas every day. On the map of Europe at the beginning I've coloured all the countries I've been to with a bright green highlighter pen. I started doing that years ago while we were living in France. It looks more impressive than it really is; I mean I've coloured the whole of Sweden in which looks pretty big as it's a long thin country, but in fact I've only ever been to Goteborg. The idea is to make me feel really well-travelled.

Tabi set out the words properly so it was far more easy to read.

Prof van Zanten NWI1045 Norfolk Way cascade love D

Van Zanten was a Dutch surname, I knew – so it was some person called Professor van Zanten.

'What's NWI1045?' Tabi asked me. 'Any ideas?'

'NWI's the flight code for Norwich airport,' I replied quickly. I'd seen it only a few weeks ago on the stickers round the handle of Dad's suitcase, when he'd got back from Portugal.

'Then it's a flight coming in today,' Tabi pointed out. 'You said your dad wanted to be sure you'd got his message. 10.45. This morning – have we got to be there?' She looked quickly at her watch. She'd bought the watch the February before in Switzerland when she and Miles had been skiing there, and it had embroidered flowers on the strap and the red and white Swiss flag on its face.

'It's OK, we'll make the airport easily,' I reassured her. 'It's only just gone nine now. We'll just bike there. "Surv" means surveillance of course, don't you agree? So we've got to watch him. Cool! But Norfolk Way. I know that's familiar. Oh, of course!'

'The hotel,' completed Tabi. The Norfolk Way is a large and I think rather expensive hotel in Norwich, up near the cathedral. 'He must be staying there.'

'Cascade, wow! Sounds really exciting,' said Tabi, pleased. We looked at each other.

Cascade is the word Dad always uses if he's talking about the bad guys – whether it's terrorists, or drug runners, or thieves, or anyone up to no good. It's our own family word really and I love it because it sounds like a special secret organisation.

Cascade: *a waterfall; something falling in loose waves like a waterfall.*

It's the French word for waterfall, too. Dad chose the word

24

'Cascade' as a kind of symbol for something trying to destroy fire, because Fire is our surname and water puts out fire. I'm probably not explaining that very well but the point is that 'cascade' to us means any kind of evil or negative force. We use it as a noun or an adjective, so we might say, 'He's definitely a Cascade,' or 'We have a Cascade situation here.'

'I wonder *what* Cascade plans?' said Tabi. 'Not that Uncle Leon would tell us, I suppose.'

'Well, obviously this professor is Cascade,' I said. 'He must be up to something, so we just have to keep an eye on him. We have to be at the airport when he arrives, and keep him under surveillance till Dad gets back. I guess he'll tell us a bit more about it all then.' I knew Dad wouldn't expect us to watch him twenty-four hours a day but he would expect us to take it seriously or he wouldn't have asked us in the first place.

I leant forward to switch on my computer. 'Let's check him out and see what he looks like,' I said. 'There can't be that many Professor van Zantens, can there? And if he's a professor there's probably a photo of him somewhere on the web. We can find out more details about him later – maybe even why he's coming to Norwich in the first place.'

'Better be quick, then,' said Tabi, looking at her watch again.

I typed in his name. Several things came up and it could take ages to trawl through them. There were several Dr van Zantens but only one professor, and he seemed to be on the staff of Leiden University, in the Netherlands.

'Try that link,' said Tabi, pointing to one which seemed to be something to do with seventeenth century art. It did seem quite hopeful, especially as the flights to Norwich come in from Amsterdam. About four photographs appeared, of people who'd all been to some conference or other in Copenhagen. His name was clearly under the second photograph. He was standing in what looked like an art gallery. He looked pretty ancient; he had a lot of hair but it was grey and he had quite a scruffy grey beard and was wearing old-fashioned thin-rimmed glasses. He was wearing a suit and it looked rather baggy. I thought from the way he was standing that he was probably bending over a bit, as some old people do. There was a text under the photograph about some research or other he'd been doing on a Flemish painter but I didn't bother to read that. Maybe we'd have to check it out later.

Tabi and I peered at the photograph, memorising what Professor van Zanten looked like. I thought he did look pretty distinctive so there'd be no problem picking him out in a crowd.

'And as he's old he'll stand out a bit at the airport,' Tabi said.

I knew what she meant. She didn't mean that older people didn't go to airports, but lots of the people on flights into Norwich are business people who definitely haven't got long grey beards, or else they're families with young children going on holiday.

Before we went down to fetch the bikes I took some extra cash from my desk drawer. Suppose we decided to follow Professor van Zanten in a taxi or something – that would be really cool!

6

De ontvoering *(Dutch)*

de – the

ontvoering – kidnapping

It didn't take too long to bike to the airport; most of the traffic in the mornings had eased off. I supposed people had got to their offices by now. We pedalled up Cromer Road and turned right towards the airport. The traffic lights had been in our favour nearly all the way up from the city centre. One of the airport shuttle buses arrived at the same time as us and a lot of people got off. Some of the people hadn't any luggage with them so I guessed they would be working at the airport today, maybe in the shops there or in the offices.

We chained our bikes to the fence in the short stay car park, winding the chain round the loops inside our cycle helmets too so they wouldn't get stolen. We didn't want to take the helmets into the airport building as it would make us more distinctive and an official might decide we were just hanging around there and would ask us to leave. We crossed over by the taxis and went inside to the departure lounge, looking up at the screens hanging from the ceiling to see which flights would be arriving soon. As we'd expected, Professor van Zanten's flight was one from Schiphol airport, in Amsterdam. The time was as Dad's message had told us and it was expected to arrive on time: 10.45.

'I'm going to grab a drink in the café,' I said. I'd decided it was quite thirsty work biking from the city centre. After all, some of it is uphill. It was rather busy in the airport building, both in the shop and in the café, and we had to wait while a family in front of us ordered a cooked breakfast. The queues were getting longer at the check-in desks, too. We'd chosen two of those packets of fruit drink with straws attached, and we took them to a table next to the window, which has a great view of planes taking off and landing. The family who'd been in front of us sat down at an adjacent table and the two small children who looked about four and five years old started pointing excitedly at a plane which was just leaving. Their parents were telling them what kind of plane it was. I think it was on its way to Edinburgh. I got the impression they were waiting to get one of this morning's planes themselves.

At Norwich airport you can sit and watch the planes through thick glass, in the café. At the far end of the runway there are occasionally helicopters taking off and landing too, transporting people to and from the gas platforms in the North Sea. Because it's a small airport there aren't that many planes coming in, and as they stop really close to the terminal building you can sometimes manage to see whoever it is you're meeting as they get off the plane, just before they go through the doors to collect their luggage and go through customs. The windows in the café are weird, though, because although you can see the planes clearly through them, if you're on the runway side of the glass you can't see into the café at all and everything looks dark. I guess it's the same kind of glass you get in some cars when the windows look blacked out.

I checked my purse and counted how much money was in it now I'd added a couple of notes. Tabi had treated me to the drink. Dad allows me to spend some cash on Ignis 'if it's in a good cause', as he says. It's his way of giving me extra pocket money. I was glad I'd taken a couple of notes from my drawer. It was unlikely we'd be able to follow Professor van Zanten from the airport really but at least we might be able to spot straight away who he was and that would save us having to ask awkward questions at the Norfolk Way Hotel where he was presumably staying.

A while ago, Dad had taken me to the airport and I'd had to 'meet' someone. I wasn't to let them know I was watching them, but I was to work out who they were from all the people coming through the arrivals gate into the main airport. 'Just use basic powers of observation,' he'd said. The person I'd had to identify had been a French lady. Dad hadn't given me any details at all. She'd been on the flight from Amsterdam and I'd found her alright. Actually I'd been incredibly lucky because there'd been a school party coming through who'd all been about my age and had all been talking Dutch excitedly and so there were plenty of people she couldn't possibly have been. I don't know if Dad had known in advance about the group. There'd only been two ladies travelling by themselves and one of them had just looked completely English somehow, particularly her shoes, so I'd guessed the other one, correctly as it turned out. I gathered later she'd been Monsieur Lesage the school French teacher's sister. It's amazing how much you can tell about people by studying their shoes. Tabi's really into that which I suppose is why she was on about my trainers having holes in them.

'They're coming through now,' said Tabi, nudging me. We'd not been able to see the professor as he got off the plane, as the café had got too crowded and too many people had been standing by the window. Once the plane had landed we'd left the café and gone round into the other part of the building, so we would have a good view of the people as they came through the automatic doors. Some people come through the doors almost as soon as the plane has landed, but they're the ones who only have hand luggage with them, or else they're the flight crew.

'He'll have some luggage with him,' said Tabi. She was right; we already knew that he would be staying at a hotel and it was evident from what Dad had told us that he'd be there at least until Dad arrived back in Norwich himself.

'Here are the flight crew,' I said. There were glass panels in the automatic doors and we could see as three people in uniform came towards us. The doors swung open. A couple of boys aged about eight and nine came through next, accompanied by a stewardess who was pulling along a suitcase for them. They were brothers; their parents had been waiting for them and everyone was hugging each other like mad. Then the stewardess asked the mother to sign some papers. She'd be able to leave them to it once that had been done. It's fun travelling by yourself when you're that age. It makes you feel very grown up, but the flight crew look after you like mad and they're always really nice. They give you great things to do, especially if it's a long flight, so you don't get bored at all.

After that the stream of passengers began. I could hear several languages being spoken. It's strange really to think how many multi-lingual people live in East Anglia, although sometimes it's referred to as a forgotten corner of England. One woman rushed through in a great hurry, surprisingly quickly considering she was carrying a really heavy blue suitcase, and shot off in the direction of the taxis. There was a group of Polish men who looked like students, with backpacks. They were laughing and joking together and I wondered whether they were on holiday or lived round here.

There was no doubt at all who Professor van Zanten was when he came through. We both recognised him instantly from his photograph. I couldn't nudge Tabi as we'd deliberately moved away from each other, so the professor wouldn't see us together. Tabi was closer to the railing and I'd moved back a little further away, nearer to the machine where people put their tickets and pay before fetching their cars in the long stay or short stay car parks. But we looked in each other's direction and gave each other a quick nod. I saw Tabi taking a photo on her phone. The professor's beard seemed to have grown longer and he looked even older than I'd thought. In fact I'd have said he looked seriously old. His glasses were halfway down his nose. He was shuffling his feet as he walked and I'd been right about his bending over. His suit was rather crumpled and looked a bit too big for him. It might have been the same one that he'd been wearing when the photograph had been taken. He was carrying a very battered small brown suitcase with quite a lot of labels stuck on the outside. The suitcase looked too heavy for him to carry by himself. I felt like going forward and offering to carry it for him. It was hard to believe that he was really Cascade.

As I was thinking that, a youngish man with short brown hair wearing smart grey trousers and a very crisp white shirt stepped towards the professor, saying something. He was also wearing a dark jacket, which looked a bit bulky, as if he'd put too many things in the pocket. Quickly I moved through what had turned into a crowd to get closer, so I'd hear what was being said. I wasn't really worried that the professor would notice me; he didn't look as though he'd notice anything going on around him at all. He had a distinctly absent-minded air about him!

I got close enough to him to hear the man in the grey trousers say, 'Professor van Zanten? My name's James Conrad. Pleased to meet you.' He then said something else that I couldn't catch because at that moment the airport made an announcement over the loudspeaker system, which was something about the flight to Aberdeen being delayed. Tabi was standing closer so I hoped she'd heard. I took my notebook out of the inside pocket of my jacket and wrote down exactly what I'd just heard this James Conrad person say. I scrawled down what he was wearing, too. That would be good to tell Dad eventually. What I hadn't bargained for was the professor's reaction to James Conrad.

'But I expected no-one at all,' he was saying in rather a shaky voice. He was speaking in English but had quite a strong Dutch accent. He sounded very surprised. 'No-one at all... at all. And you are who, you said who, young man?' he added, stopping completely, putting down his suitcase, and cupping his hand behind his ear. He looked very confused, and he turned his head towards James Conrad. When he cupped his hand I noticed he'd got a scar on it, not unlike the one I've got, only his was on his right hand.

By now the other people on the flight all seemed to have come through the automatic doors and there were only a few people left around the professor and James Conrad. No-one seemed particularly interested in them. Tabi had taken another photo, this time of James Conrad. Both Tabi and I moved away so as not to draw attention to ourselves, she towards the main exit where she logically assumed the two men would be going, and myself a little further away, in the direction of the information desk.

I pulled my mobile phone out quickly and keyed in Tabi's number. It'd be best to communicate that way from now on. There were so many people in the main hall of the airport at this time of day that we didn't look unusual; plenty of people were having conversations on their phones.

'He's taken Zanto by the arm,' Tabi hissed. 'Coming your way! And Connie's carrying the suitcase now!' Typical Tabi. She's always making up 'alternative' versions of people's names. 'Connie' instead of Conrad was typical of her. And 'Zanto'! That did sound rather good. And at least no one would ever guess who we were talking about if they overheard!

I knelt down, fiddling with my trainers, to stay out of sight behind a group of people with a collection of suitcases and bags who were discussing whether to check in yet. The professor was coming into view, but he was walking very slowly and James Conrad was almost having to hold him up. I was beginning to feel quite sorry for him. He was trying to say something to James Conrad, who didn't seem to be listening, although the professor had started to lean quite heavily against him. 'Connie' was trying to hurry him along a little. After they'd passed me I stood up. Now I could see where they were going. They were heading for the toilets.

'Loo stop,' I pronounced quietly into the phone to Tabi. 'And Zanto looks a bit past it.'

'OK, understood,' she replied straight away. 'I'll wait outside. That'll give me a few minutes to grab my bike. You stay on the look-out there.' That made sense. It's better to split up some of the time while you're carrying out surveillance, to allow for unexpected circumstances.

The professor and James Conrad had disappeared round the corner of the corridor to the toilets, and I knew there wasn't any way out down there. I'd just wait and see what happened when they reappeared. I imagined Tabi unlocking our bikes and helmets. She'd have them ready outside the airport, on the other side of the road in the car park. It seemed pretty likely that 'Connie' would have a car waiting for the professor, since he'd come specially to meet him.

When I'd been hanging around for a few minutes and had written down a few more notes, there was another announcement over the loudspeakers about a flight to Corfu, and a few people moved over to go through the turnstiles into the departure lounge. I noticed the family who had been sitting next to us in the café heading in that direction too.

My phone shook in my jacket. That would be Tabi again. 'Got him!' she said. 'Where are you? Hurry up!' What could she mean?

Got who? She couldn't mean the professor as he hadn't reappeared and there was no way he could have got past me, because I had definitely been watching for him and Connie all the time.

'Zanto!' answered Tabi impatiently. 'The professor! He's going over to the taxis. Come on! Why aren't you here?' She sounded really stressed now.

'He's still here, in the toilets, I know he is!' I said.

'He's here, dumbo, he's getting into a taxi,' Tabi said crossly. 'Don't know what happened to Connie, though. Honestly, Ninian, you must have missed him. And now I don't know what he said to the taxi driver.'

'We know the name of his hotel already,' I said. 'No panic – but...'

'I'm following!' said Tabi, sounding very fed up. 'Do what you like. Your bike's here so get it quick. Out.' 'Out' meant she was switching her phone off. She'd be on her bike now, following the taxi for as long as possible. If the traffic was slow, she'd probably be able to follow it all the way to the Norfolk Way Hotel, in the centre of the city – as long as that was where the taxi had been told to go.

I began to feel a bit stupid, toilet-watching. And now Tabi was really mad at me. Yet I knew, I just knew, that I hadn't missed the professor coming away from them. He *must* still be in there. Several people had been going round into the toilets, and coming out again. I'd been watching them all the time.

Now a woman in stewardess uniform appeared, pushing someone in a wheelchair. She was manipulating the wheelchair carefully round the corner so it wouldn't knock into the wall. The person in the wheelchair was wrapped up so completely in a blanket that I couldn't even see if it was a man or a woman. Whoever it was, they were slumped right down in the chair. It looked as though there was something bulky, like a box, on the person's knees under the blanket, which surely must be a bit uncomfortable if it was heavy. The stewardess was leaning forward, saying something to the invalid. I looked a little more closely. Wait a minute! I could see the beginning of a grey beard protruding from the blanket round the face. Surely it couldn't be... and as I watched in astonishment, the right hand of the unknown person flopped down from under the blanket. I could see a scar, very like mine but on the other hand. The stewardess tucked the hand quickly back under the blanket.

It was Professor van Zanten! Zanto! He wasn't Cascade at all! Cascade had been after him! He must have been drugged, and now he'd been kidnapped! Where was the stewardess taking him? What was going to happen to him? Who on earth was Tabi following? What had happened to James Conrad?

And most important of all, what should I do next?

7

Taxi: *a vehicle licensed to carry passengers to a specified
destination on request*

'Think logically, Ninian,' I told myself. 'Forget about Tabi and
whoever she's following because she'll deal with that and tell you
later.'

It flashed briefly into my mind that one thing I could do would
be to go over to the information desk and say something like,
'That's Professor van Zanten in the wheelchair, and I think he's
been kidnapped.' I could just imagine the disbelief, and by the time
they'd stopped telling me off and probably escorting me out of the
building, the stewardess and the professor would have disappeared
completely. I'd have no idea at all where he'd gone, and worse still I
might have messed up any plans that Dad might have for once he'd
got home. After all, he hadn't given us any background information.
He might not be too pleased if I blew everything the minute the
professor arrived!

I decided it was vital to follow them. There must be someone else
pretending to be the professor, though goodness knows why, and
they must look so like him that they'd fooled Tabi. Well, I'd find out
what was going to happen to the real one! It was a pity that I didn't
know where James Conrad had gone, but that couldn't be helped.

The stewardess was now pushing the wheelchair through the
door outside and a couple of people entering the building stood
aside for her to pass. She went over to the parking ticket machine

and I watched while she put in a ticket and some coins. No-one seemed bothered about the muffled-up person in the wheelchair. I'd now got a photo of them both on my phone.

I saw my bike leaning against the hedge by the first parked cars, where Tabi had left it. She'd taken her chain but the bike itself was locked. Should I try to follow on my bike? The woman was obviously going to get into a car. I had to decide quickly. I thought about the extra money I'd taken before leaving home. Yes, I'd go for it – I'd follow in a taxi! At last! Secretly, I'd always wanted to leap into a taxi like they do in films and say authoritatively, 'Follow that car!'

I snatched my helmet from where Tabi had left it on the saddle, deciding to risk leaving the bike itself at the airport. There were plenty of taxis waiting so I wouldn't have to queue for one.

By now the stewardess had reached a white Renault car and was opening a door. She was lifting the professor into the back seat. She must have been quite a bit stronger than she looked. Although the professor was quite short he must weigh quite a lot. Oh no, he couldn't be... dead... was he? But as that occurred to me I saw his legs move and he shakily took hold of the car door as she more or less shovelled him in. So he must be drugged, as I'd thought at first. Moving behind a couple of parked cars I memorised the Renault's number plate, ready to run to the taxis as soon as she started the engine.

The stewardess obviously didn't care if the now empty wheelchair was going to get in anyone's way. It looked as if she was just going to dump it in the car park, and already it had rolled slightly away from the car. I wasn't sure whether wheelchairs usually had brakes but if so this one hadn't got them on. As soon as she'd finished bundling the professor into the Renault, she slammed the door and almost ran to the driver's side. She got in very fast and reversed out of the parking space. I ran quickly back to the taxis.

Behind me in the car park I heard a screech of brakes and a metallic crunch. The wheelchair *had* been in someone's way!

I signalled to the driver of the taxi at the front of the line, opened the door, swung myself in and sat down on the back seat, putting my cycle helmet on the seat next to me. The driver didn't seem bothered I didn't have any luggage. He started the engine and we were already moving off.

'Where to?' he asked over his shoulder. We'd swung round the corner away from the airport building, and the white Renault had just come out of the car park, a few metres in front of us.

'Follow that car!' I said with great satisfaction.

8

Do not let your prey spot you. Observe your prey carefully so you
can predict their next move. Think before you act.

Unfortunately the driver didn't seem to like my saying that very
much.

'Look here, mate,' he said, glancing back at me. 'If you're fooling
around with me there'll be trouble. Just tell me where you want to
go, and otherwise I'll be round that roundabout and back at the
airport before you can say 'James Bond.'

'Yea, um, sorry,' I said, thinking quickly. 'I do know the people in
the car and it's, um, a kind of game we're playing but they mustn't
see I'm following them.'

'Hm,' said the driver. I'd put on my most polite voice and it
sounded as though it might be working.

'I can pay you, really,' I said, holding up the notes I'd taken from
home.

'Well...' replied the driver, as we pulled into Cromer Road in the
direction of the city centre. It seemed as if showing him the money
had helped. 'I've got to tell my boss something, you know – I mean,
I can't just drive round in circles.'

'I think they're going to a hotel in town,' I told him desperately.

'Right,' said the driver in a rather more friendly voice. 'I'll tell my
boss we're going to the train station – but if we end up going further
than that and you can't tell me where, then that's it and I drop you
off and you pay, understand?'

'Fine,' I agreed, and he spoke briefly into his phone.

There was now a blue van between us and the Renault, but it did seem that the taxi driver was keeping at a suitable distance. At the traffic lights the Renault turned left along the main road and after a few minutes I saw that the route it was taking was towards Wroxham. It wouldn't be long before the driver started complaining and I'd have to get out or give up and go back to the airport with him. I was looking out of the window all the time, checking that the Renault was still there but also desperately trying to remember where we were. We were going further away from the city all the time and soon there would only be countryside around us. There were trees on each side of the road now.

Just as the driver was starting to say, 'Right, mate, I can't take you any further,' the Renault indicated that it was going to turn left. There was a wooden sign saying 'Kingfisher Cabins' and a picture of a kingfisher was painted on it.

'This is it! Of course!' I said, trying to sound as if I recognised where we were. In fact I'd never heard of Kingfisher Cabins, but at least I knew what road we were on so would probably be able to get home alright, even if I had to walk.

'Thank you very much!' I said.

The Renault had disappeared up a rough track through the trees, but the taxi had been able to pull in easily in a kind of clearing by the open wooden gate, so when it had stopped I got out, remembering my cycle helmet, and went to the driver's window. I handed over a couple of notes and the driver even gave me some change back. Luckily the ride hadn't been as expensive as I'd thought. It had felt as though we'd been travelling for ages.

'Good luck, mate!' the driver said, giving a friendly wave before he turned the car and sped back the way we'd come. Now I was on my own!

Instead of walking up the track I decided to keep to the bushes at the side, in case anyone came along. I guessed there would be some kind of office at the end where people had to go when they arrived. After a couple of minutes I could see that the Renault was parked by a wooden cabin. Another car was parked there too. There was a sign on the cabin saying 'Reception'. I could see that 'Zanto' was sitting in the back of the car, and his head was slumped forward. The cabin door was open and I could see the stewardess inside, standing by a desk. I crept round to the side of the cabin. The window there was slightly ajar.

' ...and your uncle, of course,' I heard a woman's voice say. 'Welcome to Kingfisher Cabins.' There was a murmur of more conversation but I couldn't hear it properly.

Then another voice, which must have been the stewardess, said, 'As I explained in my email, my uncle is subject to mental relapses.' I wondered what that meant. It didn't sound good. 'We do not wish to be disturbed at all. At all!' she emphasised and her voice had a very nasty edge to it as though in fact it was a threat. It gave me rather a creepy feeling and I looked round to check no-one else was listening. At that moment the trees and bushes round me didn't feel very friendly at all. It was almost as if they were moving in on me. I shivered a little. What a Cascade woman! She really gave me the creeps.

'He is recovering from a serious mental illness,' she continued. 'He really must not be disturbed AT ALL.'

'Of course, certainly,' the other voice said, sounding almost frightened as well. I didn't dare to go closer to the window to see who the other person was. The conversation continued a little longer and I gathered that the stewardess had booked cabin number two in the woods for a week and she'd arranged for it to be well stocked with food and drink. She was definitely planning to stay for a while.

I didn't dare to go to the car to check on Professor van Zanten but at least it sounded as though he was going to be kept alive. Cascade must have chosen this place to keep him hidden for a few days, while the other person, who Tabi was following, pretended to be him in Norwich. But why?

A few minutes later the Renault was parked outside cabin two, a small low building hidden away among some trees quite a long way behind the reception building. It was rather like a caravan but made of wood. I'd been able to see the professor stagger into the cabin himself so at least that was something. The stewardess had carried his suitcase in after him together with another bag, which must have been in the car all the time. Now there was the sound of things being moved around and cupboards being opened and closed.

I debated what to do. It sounded as though the Cascade plan was to remain here, so what good could it do for me to stay any longer? Should I somehow try to help the professor? But I could hardly do that while the stewardess was there. I retreated further into the trees, rather clumsily tripping over a tree root. I hoped no-one heard me as I fell. Luckily no-one else seemed to be about at all, though I could faintly hear the traffic on the main road. It wasn't as warm as it had been and it occurred to me it might be going to rain. The sky was definitely getting greyer. I called up Tabi but her phone was switched off. I guessed she was still fed up with me.

'I know,' I said to myself. 'I'll risk trying to see into the cabin, and then I'll go home. At least I know where he is now. Not much else I can do.'

Carefully I approached the back of the cabin, away from the track where the car was parked. The bushes continued till almost up to the building. I kept right down below the level of the windows. I didn't think I'd leave any footprints in the grass and leaves. The woman inside said something and her voice came from my left, away from the window I'd got to, so I stood up slowly, holding my breath, and peeped into the cabin.

The professor was lying on a bed with his eyes closed, but he looked comfortable and there was a mug on a table next to him which might have contained coffee, or tea. On the floor I could see his suitcase had been opened and a few clothes were lying next to it. The stewardess was at the far end of the room with her back to me. She was putting something into a cupboard. I craned my neck to look further in but nothing else caught my eye. It did look as though they were here to stay. I ducked down again, moved as silently as I could away from the building, and went back through the woods to the track and then the road.

I thought of the training Dad had given us on surveillance. He'd had fun giving us that. *'Do not let your prey spot you.'* They hadn't, which was vital. *'Observe your prey carefully so you can predict their next move.'* Yes, I'd observed them alright, and they'd be staying at Kingfisher Cabins. *'Think before you act.'* Well, there was plenty of thinking to do, and some of it needed to be done with Tabi. I'd get back to Norwich – and that looked like being a long walk!

9

Doppelgänger *(German)*

Doppelgänger – someone's mysterious look-alike; a ghost-like apparition that resembles someone

After reaching the main road I'd walked for about a hundred metres back towards Norwich and then found myself next to a bus stop. It had been a long wait, but finally a bus had come along saying 'City', so I'd got on and it had dropped me off near the airport. My bike was still there waiting for me, thank goodness. I'd been right about the rain; there was a massive downpour and by the time I'd got home I was completely drenched. When I'd changed and made myself a very late lunch of a sandwich, fruit and a few biscuits, I'd managed to get hold of Tabi on my mobile and calm her down. She'd come over to my place, walking along the few streets from her house under a giant spotty umbrella. She's the only person our sort of age that I know who ever uses an umbrella. She says it's because an umbrella is an accessory and she likes co-ordinating accessories. I'm not really sure what she's on about.

Anyway, once she'd seen the photos on my phone and I'd seen her photo of who she'd been following there was no question about it; there were two professors.

'There's a name for that, you know,' Tabi said excitedly. 'It's a doppelgänger – some weird double, who looks exactly the same as someone else. So Zanto's got a doppelgänger.' She was saying the word in German, which is what it is in English too if you see what I mean.

I remembered seeing a little bit of a very scary film once about someone who'd seen their own 'doppelgänger'. They'd been looking into a shop window and then caught sight of their reflection, and there had been someone just like them standing about a metre behind them. Understandably, it had really freaked them out. I think I'd certainly go crazy if I had an experience like that. Mind you, Dad and Uncle Paul have some very funny stories about how they used to play tricks on people when they were little – people who hadn't realised they were identical twins.

Tabi had followed the man she'd thought was Professor van Zanten all the way to the Norfolk Way Hotel. He'd checked in and she'd left him there. 'He's staying in room 127,' she said. 'So we know where to find him. But who do you think Doppy really is?' There she went again. 'Doppy' – short for doppelgänger, of course. And we agreed that the person pretending to be Professor van Zanten was Cascade, and that the real professor must be completely innocent. It would have helped if Dad's message had been clearer.

'There must be something important about to happen to Zanto,' I said. 'I mean, there must be a good reason for him to be in Norwich in the first place. And maybe he's supposed to meet someone and get given secret information. Only he won't get that information because Doppy will get it instead.'

'Wow, Ninian, I bet that's it,' said Tabi, nodding slowly. 'And then Cascade will have that information and do something terrible with it. And Zanto will just have to go home without it.'

'Which means that he will just be allowed to go once Cascade have the information,' I said. 'At least, I hope so.' I was still feeling very sorry for the real Professor van Zanten, shut up in a cabin with that stewardess. He must be wondering what on earth was going on. I wished I'd been able to rescue him.

'Well, at least we know where he is too,' said Tabi. 'From what you saw, that stewardess or whatever is looking after him, and if she'd been going to shoot him or something they'd have done it by now, wouldn't she, not bother to keep him hidden away.' I agreed with her. That did make sense. And once Dad got back we'd be able to tell him where Kingfisher Cabins was and he'd make sure the professor was rescued. Tabi must have been starting to mind-read.

'When is your dad coming back?' she asked me.

'At the end of the week,' I said. 'He'll be flying into Norwich. He may even have started travelling by now.' I wasn't sure what route Dad was taking back from China, as it depended on whether he was going to stop off somewhere like Singapore on the way back. I didn't see any point in trying to get a message to him about what we'd found out. We could tell him exactly what we'd seen soon enough. And I wanted to find out more about Cascade before he came home. Surely he couldn't have known that Cascade had planned to kidnap Professor van Zanten as soon as he arrived at the airport? Otherwise surely he'd have warned the police, and not let us get involved at all.

'I guess he thought Cascade wouldn't do anything till he got back, and it would just be good for us to keep an eye on things,' said Tabi. There she was, mind-reading again.

'Definitely,' I replied. 'But I wish I knew what Cascade's planning. What can be so important about the professor? Do you think he's made some scientific discovery?'

'You know what we could do?' said Tabi suddenly. 'If you're up for it that is.'

'What?' I asked.

'Well, we could sneak into Doppy's hotel room when he's not there, and have a look around,' she said. 'He might have left some important papers there or something. He can hardly just sit there in his room all day. He'll have to go out for meals and things. Then perhaps we can find something out.'

'That's a great idea!' I agreed. 'Why don't we do that now?' I thought I sounded quite cool about it, but did wonder how we were going to manage that. And suppose we got caught? Still, I wasn't going to let Tabi know I felt like that.

As we went into the hall downstairs and down the steps into the street we could see that the rain had stopped and the sky was starting to clear, and there was that clean wet smell in the air that there always is after a downpour. Tabi had taken her umbrella from by the front door and rolled it up. It was still quite cool outside and I put my jacket on. There was a vague murmur of voices from the classrooms; afternoon language classes were in full swing. That reminded me, Mum had asked me to tidy up the classrooms every evening this week, ready for the next day's lessons.

It only took us a few minutes to walk up to the Norfolk Way Hotel. It was at a crossroads, near to the cathedral. It had a large car park round the back, and at the front you went in through glass doors leading to a reception area. Further down the side of the building there was another entrance, into a restaurant which belonged to the hotel too.

'I hope it's not the same woman at reception,' said Tabi anxiously as we approached. 'She's going to think it's a bit weird if I start hanging round again. I had a job to find out what room Zanto's in.' But we were in luck. A man was standing behind the desk, talking to a couple of people who looked as though they were checking in. They'd got a couple of bags and a suitcase on the floor next to them. The man behind the desk was wearing a name badge and as we got closer I could see his name was Rory. So Tabi wouldn't be recognised. The woman who had been at the desk must have gone home.

Just then we heard a coach drawing up outside. Some more of the hotel staff appeared as though from nowhere at the reception desk. A large crowd of people started coming in through the doors, and more were gathering on the pavement outside. It looked as though a whole group of tourists were arriving. It was easy for Tabi and me to move closer to the desk without anyone taking any notice of us.

'Look,' whispered Tabi. 'His key's on the hook, so that means he's out. You have to hand your key in when you leave the hotel.' She was pointing behind Rory's head and I could see a large board fixed to the wall. There were lots of hooks on it and each hook was numbered. Many of them had gold coloured keys with gold coloured fobs hanging from them. The second row of hooks had one numbered 127, and there was a gold key on it.

'Oh well,' I said. 'We'd better...' but suddenly I froze. I'd turned away from the desk and among the people coming into the hotel I saw a grey head approaching. It was definitely the man pretending to be the professor! The doppelgänger! There wasn't time to say anything, but I pulled Tabi's sleeve and we moved quickly behind an armchair. Luckily the people from the coach were still forming a crowd. 'Doppy' went straight to the desk, to ask for his key. He had to wait for a couple of minutes as the hotel staff were helping the newcomers.

'Look at his shoes,' hissed Tabi. 'Just the same – see?' Trust her to notice, but in fact I'd remembered the shoes that the real professor had been wearing too. They'd been brown leather ones with a pattern of holes punched in the leather. I think they're called brogues. This man did look very like the professor, but he wasn't bent over so much and his beard wasn't as long. Now I knew it wasn't really him I realised that the hair and beard could easily be a wig. The hair was a bit too thick really for someone supposed to be that old; with old men you can always see where the hair's gone thin, or they have bald patches – if they haven't gone completely bald, that is. I felt my own hair. There was plenty of that, anyway. Your head must get cold when you're going bald, I thought. It was strange to think that one day I might go bald too.

His glasses were like the professor's too, but they were so far down his nose that he probably wasn't actually looking through them at all. And the suit he was wearing was the same colour as the professor's but less baggy, somehow. It looked cleaner, too, though rather crumpled. 'Doppy' was carrying a briefcase, one of those old-fashioned brown leather ones that contain papers and files and books. They're the wrong shape inside for laptops. I wondered what was inside.

'Oh, Professor van Zanten,' said Rory, reaching for the key to room number 127. 'There's a message for you. It was delivered about half an hour ago. I believe your meeting has been changed to tomorrow afternoon.' He took an envelope from the shelf behind him and gave it to 'Doppy', who grunted his thanks and took both the key and the envelope. Then he moved towards the lift and entered it with a couple of other people. There was a 'ping' sound as the doors closed, and then a hum as the lift went up.

'Well!' said Tabi. 'We have just got to find out what that letter says!'

'That's easily said,' I replied. 'Any ideas on how we do that?' The reception area had cleared now and there weren't so many people about. I glanced round. Next to the lift was a flight of stairs going up to the first floor. Down it was coming a woman in a grey overall, carrying a couple of sheets.

'Of course!' exclaimed Tabi. 'Room service! We'll get into Doppy's room tomorrow morning, when they're cleaning the bedrooms after breakfast!' Before I could stop her she went up to the desk where

Rory was straightening things on the counter. 'Excuse me,' she said. 'Could you tell me what time breakfast is served tomorrow?'

'Certainly,' said Rory. 'From seven thirty to nine.' Tabi came back to where I was by the exit.

'You see!' she said proudly. 'He'll have to go out while they clean his room. And then we'll get in! It'll be easy!'

I was a bit annoyed she'd let Rory notice her by asking him a question. Not that he'd probably remember. But as for getting into room 127... personally I didn't think it sounded easy at all. However I did agree that we had to try.

10

Selim morf egassem *(code message)*

When I got home it was nearly supper time. Mum was in the kitchen cooking. I remembered to ask her how the new students had got on; it's quite stressful for her making sure everything goes smoothly on the days that new ones arrive.

'Oh, it went fine, thanks, Ninian,' she said. 'One or two arrived late, Janet said, but basically everything went according to plan. They seem to have got off to a good start.'

'D'you want me to tidy the classrooms this evening?' I asked.

'Yes, please, if you would,' she replied. 'Could you wait till after half past eight – the last lesson this evening finishes then.'

'Sure,' I said. I laid the table and helped Mum to get the rest of the supper ready. It was sausages and beefburgers, with bread rolls and salad. There was the rest of yesterday's apple pie for pudding.

At about a quarter to nine I went downstairs to the classrooms and tidied them up. In one of the classrooms I had to clean the board. There was a lot of writing on it; there were things like 'beginnen – begon – begonnen' and 'nehmen – nam – genommen' so I knew that in that class the students had been learning German verbs.

By the time I was back in my room I was about to check my emails when my phone went off; it was a message from Miles. I remembered he'd gone to stay with his friend Colin. He'd written in code; I copied it onto a piece of paper so I could look at it properly.

HUIECIOVLSIMNMAMNPDOIRFPOWLELIOMWRENDKTPHVOWRL
TIOEDUAQYNBHUMTFLIOCSETRHUINMPIGNVTEOEWJNMHAOW
PQEWUVDLOCNXTZMWIFNRDNBKUHTMHCAMVYEGNBTCTPOLL
UDBCROILKIMNHAQBVOLUITYIMGHNUIBSWCXUXTYOLMPOURE
REOQWIMNIGLWEAS

A letter code – and it must have taken Miles a long time to get down! It would have been quicker to email it to me, I thought. I looked at it carefully. I was pretty sure there were a lot of random letters in it and there weren't any numbers.

Starting at the beginning, I looked to see if it was clear what letters I should miss out. Perhaps some words were obvious. H, two letters, E – that would spell 'he' which might be the first word. O – S – N. No. It was a long message for Miles to have sent, so probably the code was simple. Of course – it was just every other letter that mattered. That was it. It started with 'Hi.'

HICOLINANDIFOLLOWEDTHORTODAYBUTLOSTHIMINTOWN
HOPEUDONTMINDBUTHAVENTTOLDCOLINABOUTIGNISCU
TOMORROWMILES

Now I was able to read what it said, without having to write anything down. I didn't really mind him following Thor, as long as he did it carefully. And Miles had already promised ages ago not to tell anyone about Ignis. But perhaps it was just as well Miles didn't know what we'd got involved with now, specially as Dad had told me not to get him scared. It was probably much better that he was just having fun with Colin.

I sent a quick reply as it was getting late. Miles would be hoping I would.

'A demain' means 'till tomorrow' in French; I thought Miles would know that, and if he didn't he could look it up. I'd needed to write the message down before I sent it; spelling's sometimes tricky when you're writing words backwards.

When I'd done that I realised I was pretty tired. It had been a long day and getting soaked earlier in the day hadn't helped. And I'd promised Tabi I'd be outside the Norfolk Way Hotel at eight o'clock tomorrow morning. That way we'd know when 'Doppy' went out – and we'd get into his room. If Tabi's plan worked.

I went to bed.

11

De brief *(Dutch)*
de – the
brief – letter

I didn't sleep well that night. I kept having short snatches of dream in which I was in the cabin with Professor van Zanten, trying to get him out, while at the same time I knew that the stewardess, James Conrad and the doppelgänger were outside among the trees waiting to catch us. In the dream I was talking to the professor in Dutch, while everyone outside was shouting in English. It was a really weird dream.

Still, I was sitting on a wall by some railings near the Norfolk Way Hotel the next morning a couple of minutes before Tabi arrived, and was able to give her the impression I'd been waiting for her for ages.

'Oh, sorry I'm a bit late, Ninian,' she said, glancing at her watch. She was carrying a striped shoulder bag. The stripes were those candy colours of pink and blue. 'Miles says thanks for your message. Let's go round the back by the car park,' she continued. 'Then you can help me.'

I'd no idea what she was planning but as long as she did have some kind of plan I wasn't going to complain. I still didn't really see how we could get into the doppelgänger's room without a key – and certainly no-one was going to give us one!

We went round the corner and stood by some of those large industrial dustbins, the kind that are too big to lift or push along by yourself. They had 'Norfolk Way' printed on them in rather dirty white letters. Near us was a door into the hotel and there was the smell of cooked breakfasts wafting out. I'd only just had breakfast but I could have eaten some sausages. These ones smelt delicious!

Tabi opened her shoulder bag and pulled out some material. When she unfolded it I saw it was a white coat, the kind people wear in laboratories or hospitals over their clothes, as a sort of uniform.

'Mum wears these sometimes when she's delivering food to parties,' she said. 'She's got a couple of them so she won't notice I've borrowed this one. Hold my bag while I put it on.'

She took her jacket off and gave it to me. I stuffed it into her bag while she was putting on the white coat. Now I began to understand! The coat was a little long for her but she did look as though she might be working in the hotel, cleaning or something. She certainly looked more efficient. I noticed she wasn't wearing her trainers but had put on smarter shoes. I thought her face might look a bit too young to work here but that probably wasn't important. I was beginning to feel this might actually work!

'Listen,' Tabi said. 'You nip round and wait till Doppy leaves the hotel. I'll wait here, out of sight. Then get back here and we'll go in the back way and upstairs to his room. I'll need you to help.'

I wasn't going to argue as she'd obviously thought this through. I didn't go into the hotel as there was no need for now; better to make sure no-one noticed me. I crossed the road where I could sit on another piece of wall, with my back against some railings. I guess I looked as though I was waiting for some friends. I wondered how long I'd have to wait, and was glad it wasn't raining like it had been yesterday. Quite a few guests were already coming out of the hotel and a lot of people seemed to be gathering inside the foyer, near the doors.

Luckily I didn't have to wait very long in the end before the doppelgänger came out and set off down the hill towards the city centre. He was carrying the brown briefcase in his left hand, and I'd have given a lot to know what was in it. He was walking pretty fast, considering how old he was supposed to be. I was quite sure by now that he was a much younger man than the real Professor van Zanten. I wished I could follow him now, but Tabi had said she'd need my help in the hotel. And it would be brilliant if we could find something important in the doppelgänger's room!

I was about to cross over when a coach pulled over in front of the hotel, blocking my view of the reception desk and the entrance doors. On the side of the coach there was 'Norfolk Broads day tours' written in large green letters, and round the lettering there were pictures of boats and birds. It must have come to collect some guests to take them out for the day. As I passed it to get to the car park the driver got out and said to a woman on the pavement, 'I'm a bit early, love. We don't leave for another twenty minutes.' He walked through the main doors into the hotel.

Tabi was waiting where I'd left her.

'He's left,' I told her. 'Looked as if was going into the city centre. He's carrying the briefcase.'

'Right, good,' she said. She was looking quite fierce and was obviously determined her plan was going to work. 'What's that coach doing?' she asked. The front of the coach could be seen sticking round the corner.

'I think they're fetching people for a day trip,' I answered. 'The driver says they're not leaving yet.'

'Oh, perfect,' she said, and her face went thoughtful. She was obviously fitting that information into her plan in some way. 'Come on, we'll go through here.' I felt a bit stupid carrying her stripy shoulder bag with the jacket in it, but I could hardly leave it outside in case someone chucked it in one of the dustbins. I bundled it under my arm.

We slipped inside through the side door and saw a large kitchen on our left. There was still a fantastic breakfast smell. A man with striped trousers and a white coat had his back to us and was loading plates into an enormous dishwasher. He was making quite a lot of noise and luckily he didn't turn round as we nipped past him. A fire door was ahead of us and through its glass panel we could see a flight of stairs going up. I pointed silently. We pulled the door open and ran quickly up before anyone saw us.

Since the doppelgänger's room number was 127 we knew his room had to be on the first floor. With hotel rooms the first number is the floor of the building. So there were at least twenty-seven rooms on the first floor of this hotel. At the top of the flight of stairs the floor was carpeted and the whole atmosphere was smart and expensive, although it was rather stuffy. Here it smelt of air freshener instead of breakfasts.

Tabi was pretending to be working at the hotel; my excuse would have to be that I was a guest. I moved a bit away from Tabi and tried to look more confident, as though I was definitely allowed to be walking along the first floor corridor. Tabi was searching the doors, trying to find the right number. She pointed to one on the right. She'd found it – number one hundred and twenty-seven. As I was wondering what the next part of her plan was, there was the clank of something at the end of the corridor. A chambermaid appeared, pushing a trolley heaped with towels, sheets and some cleaning materials. She must be going to clean these rooms.

'You hide, I'll talk,' hissed Tabi quickly. I nipped round the next corner. Someone came out of a door next to me but I don't think they even noticed me. I pretended to be studying a map on the wall.

It was one of East Anglia and was in a glass frame, like a poster. I could hear Tabi talking to someone. It must be the chambermaid.

'Could you open this room first, please?' I heard Tabi's voice say. 'The guest has forgotten his coat and he's about to leave on the day trip. I'm supposed to fetch it for him. He's very old,' she added.

Wow, Tabi sounded so confident. It was really impressive! Well, I knew she was a pretty good actress. I could imagine the friendly smile she was putting on. And thanks to the white coat the chambermaid must have assumed she did work for the hotel. I heard a clink of keys. It had been easy! It was working!

'I'll be at that room in about five minutes,' I heard the chambermaid say. That gave us a bit of time! My mobile shook and I flapped it open.

'I'm in!' hissed Tabi. 'Keep watch there and tell me if anyone else comes. I've only got a couple of minutes!'

A few people came along the corridor, going towards the stairs. One of them said, 'Good morning,' to me, definitely assuming I was a guest too. I walked along the corridor past the room Tabi was in. She'd left the door open but I couldn't see her. I could see a shirt draped over the back of a chair. The trolley was parked in the corridor a few doors down; the chambermaid came out of a bedroom and went into the next. Now she was in the room next door! Tabi would have to be quick!

Suddenly Tabi appeared in the doorway.

'Quick, Ninian! Have a look at this and memorise it too. I need to put it back!' she whispered, and gave me what looked like a letter, written on pale yellow paper. She was holding the envelope. I'm a quick reader. I took it and skimmed the contents. There was an address at the top of the paper, so I could see that the letter was from something called the East Anglian Institute of sixteenth century art.

58

'Dear Professor van Zanten,' it read. 'I do hope you have settled comfortably into your hotel. As you know we had arranged for the Heffinck papers to be brought to you this coming Friday, but unfortunately Professor Rose has to return to London earlier than he expected. I shall therefore deliver the papers to your hotel myself on Tuesday 19th at 1.30 pm. If this time is not convenient to you please contact me by email or phone the above number. Very best wishes, Marjorie Fox.'

Tabi was holding out her hand, waiting for me to finish. I thrust it back at her. I was really worried that the chambermaid would reappear at any moment. It had been a brilliant idea of Tabi's to pretend someone had left their coat in the room but it wouldn't be so brilliant if we were found in there together without a coat in sight!

Luckily Tabi was back quickly, and she pulled the door shut behind her. We ran round the corner, not daring to look behind us to see if the chambermaid had spotted us. I didn't hear the trolley move, so I suppose she was still in the room next to the professor's. I was going to go back down the stairs we'd come up, but Tabi stopped me. She was taking off the white coat and rolling it up.

'Main stairs,' she said as she rolled the coat up and took her jacket from the shoulder bag. 'We're guests now, right?'

As we returned downstairs and went into the foyer we could see that a group of people were getting into the coach, ready to go on their Broads trip. No-one noticed us slipping through the door, and soon we were making our way down towards the city centre, the way that the doppelgänger had gone.

'I found the letter in the drawer by his bed,' explained Tabi. 'I've put it back and I don't think he'll notice. I've put it back in the envelope.'

'You were brilliant,' I told her admiringly. 'Fantastic. We'd never have got in there without your plan.' I really meant it. She certainly had a lot of nerve! Tabi looked pleased.

'Well, we were lucky the chambermaid was there. It was scary, though. I thought someone else might come past and see me. But I'm not going in there again! It was weird, though,' she added. 'There was hardly anything there, in the room I mean. A few clothes, but it didn't even look as if the bed had been slept in.'

We discussed what had been in the letter.

'Heffinck papers,' I pondered. 'It said sixteenth century art, so I suppose Heffinck must be one of the artists. It looks like a Belgian name, with 'nck' at the end – and there were all those links with Norfolk and the Netherlands and Belgium in the sixteenth century, weren't there?' I remembered reading about that at Norwich museum in the castle – all about the wool trade with Belgium, and Dutch painters. It's one of the reasons so many people in Norfolk have surnames that sound Dutch. Their ancestors moved here from across the North Sea because there was so much trading going on. And it's why there are lots of houses with Dutch-looking gables; Dutch people built them.

'So I suppose he must be giving a lecture about it all or something,' I continued. 'But why does Cascade want the papers? They must be pretty important to have to keep the real Professor van Zanten out of the way. Perhaps this Heffinck person wrote them. Do you think they're worth a lot of money?'

'I've no idea,' answered Tabi. ' But somehow we've got to stop Cascade getting those papers at half past one!' I absolutely agreed. But how on earth were we going to do that?

12

Tqhwejeansvdeflpoipue *(code message)*

One thing Tabi and I agreed on was that we'd got to be back at the hotel for half past one, when this Marjorie Fox person would give the papers to the doppelgänger. We didn't see how we'd be able to get the papers – we could hardly just snatch them away from him as that would give everything away and might put the real professor at risk. We still didn't know what was going to happen to him. And there was still Dad to consider, who'd told me that this was just a surveillance task. I was quite sure he didn't want us to draw attention to ourselves.

'I wish we knew where he was going when he went off after breakfast,' I'd said on the way to her house.

'Maybe he's going to Kingfisher Cabins, to see Connie and Zanto,' said Tabi, getting out her front door key. 'They're probably discussing their next plan, for when they've got the papers.'

I knew there wasn't much point in going to check on 'Connie and Zanto' – for a start it was quite a long way out of Norwich, and also we were pretty sure that the real professor would be released once Cascade had got the papers. And we'd be able to tell Dad about them soon. There was no way we could rescue the professor ourselves.

'Miles is coming back today from Colin's,' Tabi said. 'And Mum wants me to help her for some of this morning. She's got to do a lunch for a new office that's opened somewhere over by Chapelfield. But I'll be free in time.'

When I got home the language classes were in full swing at Phoenix. I looked down through the railings into the basement. The students were sitting at desks and seemed to be working in little groups of three of four. It was probably a conversation exercise. The tutor was Jamie; he was leaning over talking to one of the groups and they all seemed to be laughing. He teaches English for us every Easter and summer. He's my favourite of all our tutors; he's really nice and very funny. He always has great jokes and stories. The rest of the year he lives in Suffolk and I think he teaches drama there. I suppose it could be fun, having two jobs.

I went up the steps and went into Phoenix. Sharon was at her desk. 'Oh, good morning, Ninian,' she said, smiling. 'You're up bright and early. We've only just started!'

'Hullo, Sharon,' I replied. I was glad she was in a good mood. Sometimes she's quite moody and doesn't like me hanging around. I've no idea why.

'There's some post for you,' she said, and handed me a pile of envelopes. Our post comes through the door into the same letterbox as the language school.

'Thanks,' I said. 'I'll take it upstairs.'

'It'll be busy later,' she said. 'We've got a trip to the Broads this afternoon.' More trips to the Broads! I knew Mum organises voluntary afternoon or evening trips for the students sometimes; they sign up if they want to go.

'They'll like that,' I said. The Broads trips are good because you're outside a lot and get to go in a boat too. Upstairs I put the post on the kitchen table for Mum, helped myself to some biscuits, and went to my room to chill out for a while.

* * *

The good thing about living in the centre of a town is that you get everywhere easily. I do bike to school, but usually everywhere's within walking distance. So it didn't take me long to get back up to the Norfolk Way Hotel. I didn't know whether to expect the doppelgänger to be at the hotel yet or not. Not that it was important, because wherever he was now, he'd have to be here at half past one. I was a good fifteen minutes early. Tabi'd said she'd meet me here but there was no sign of her yet. I decided I'd wait for her inside, but there were no guests by the reception desk. I could see Rory standing there looking rather bored. He'd certainly notice if I went past him. Then I remembered the side door, that was the entrance to the restaurant. Quickly I went round the corner to go in that way. Just when I was going to go inside, my phone went. It was Tabi.

'Ninian,' she said. I could tell she was trying to keeping her voice down. 'It's a pain – I'm having to help Mum at this lunch thing. One of her helpers is ill. I'll be able to get away in a minute.'

'Oh,' I said, not liking the sound of things. This was going to be tricky. I'd have to manage this by myself. On the other hand, come to think of it, Tabi had been so much in charge about getting the letter from the doppelgänger's room that it was about time I was the one to do something important.

'Don't worry,' I began, worrying a bit already, but she interrupted me. 'Sorry – got to go!'

I went into the restaurant. It was really busy in there and there was a buzz of conversation. Most of the tables were taken and there was a lovely smell of roast dinner. This was certainly where a lot of the hotel guests must be. Mum had left some pretty good ham and pickle sandwiches out for me but this was much nicer, I thought, peering enviously at someone's plate piled high with slices of beef, Yorkshire pudding and gravy.

'Have you got a reservation?' a waitress asked me suddenly as I was looking around for the way through into the main hotel. I spun round. She was carrying a tray piled high with dirty plates and cutlery. 'Um, no, my parents are in the hotel,' I said, moving to the side a bit as she probably needed to get past. Did she really think I'd booked a table just for me?

'Through there,' she pointed, and I squeezed past some more tables and found myself in the back of the large hotel lounge. There were some really huge squishy armchairs, the kind you sink right into, and they were arranged in groups around low tables. It all looked very comfortable and had a kind of calm and peaceful atmosphere. There was a sort of leathery smell. At one group of armchairs there were four middle-aged people with laptops; I couldn't understand what they were saying but I did recognise it as German. They were talking in low voices, as if they were trying not to disturb anybody. I guessed they were having a business meeting.

I chose a chair where I could see both the main entrance and the stairs which the doppelgänger would come down if he was upstairs in his room at the moment. Wow, these chairs were amazing. You really did sink right into them! I'd already decided that if anyone asked me what I was doing I'd say I was waiting for my parents. I thought that as long as I looked quiet no-one would mind. Better switch my phone off, though. And I picked up a magazine from the table, flicking through it. After all, that's what you do at the dentist if you have to wait. The magazine wasn't very interesting; it was all about how to turn crummy old houses into posh modern mansions. Still, some of the 'before and after' illustrations were pretty impressive. I'd never have thought they were the same houses.

All the time I was looking at the magazine I was glancing up at the reception desk and also keeping an eye on the stairs, and it was only a couple of minutes before the doppelgänger came in from outside. He looked rather hot and bothered, as though he'd got here in a hurry from somewhere. And I still thought he moved much too fast considering he was looking so old. Old people just don't rush about like that.

He paused at the reception desk to ask Rory something and then came to sit in one of the lounge chairs, presumably to wait for Marjorie Fox. I imagined Tabi calling her 'Foxy' and smiled to myself. The doppelgänger was a couple of tables away from me and was facing the entrance; at least that meant he probably wouldn't notice me at all.

He was only just in time, because the next person coming in turned out to be Marjorie Fox herself. She was a tall woman with dark brown longish hair, wearing a long green and blue dress which came nearly to her ankles, and over the dress she was wearing a dark blue jacket. I thought of Tabi noticing shoes and made a mental note that she was wearing flat, black shoes which were slightly pointed. She looked about the same age as Mum, which is forty-three. Her hair was actually a bit like fox's fur. Maybe she'd dyed it that colour on purpose. She had a small black handbag over her shoulder and all she was carrying apart from that was a brown envelope. It was larger than the kind letters are usually in. The magazine I'd just been looking at would have fitted in it comfortably. I didn't dare get my mobile out to take a photo of her and she was too far away anyway, but I kind of knew it was Marjorie Fox even before she'd gone over to the reception desk and spoken to Rory, who indicated the doppelgänger sitting in the lounge area.

So the Heffinck papers, whatever they were, had to be inside the envelope!

13

The hand-over – to be observed

This had to be the moment Cascade – whoever Cascade were – had been waiting for. All the plans that they had made to kidnap Professor van Zanten at the airport and have someone pretend to be him had been so that they would get their hands on these papers. They had to be really valuable. And here they were, being given to the doppelgänger! This was so painful to see!

When Marjorie Fox approached the doppelgänger he began to rise from his chair, but she motioned for him to stay where he was, and sat down next to him after they had shaken hands. From the way that Marjorie Fox was talking to him I could see that she had no idea at all that he wasn't who she thought he was. She couldn't have met him before. It was so frustrating that I wasn't near enough to hear what they were saying, but I could hardly get up and go and sit next to them. Even if I did that I might not be able to hear properly; there were no seats really close and most of the time people were walking through the lounge to or from the restaurant behind me, chatting to each other.

'All I can do is watch for the moment,' I told myself. I was desperately trying to think of a plan of action. Hopefully Tabi would arrive before Marjorie Fox left. The chances were that as soon as he could, the doppelgänger would be off somewhere with the envelope and we'd never see him again. And I really didn't see what we could do about it. Worst of all, we had no idea what he really looked like, once he took his disguise off. If only I could delay him somehow. Where on earth was Tabi?

I nearly jumped out of my skin when someone tapped me on the shoulder. It was a waitress, dressed in black and wearing a white apron.

'Are you waiting for somebody?' she asked me. She didn't sound interested, just rather bored. It didn't seem as if she minded me sitting here at all.

'Um, yes, I'm waiting for my parents,' I replied. I don't like lying but I could hardly tell her I was sitting there witnessing someone giving some important papers to the wrong person.

'Would you like a drink?' she asked.

'Um, no thank you. I think they'll be here in a minute,' I replied. Of course I had no idea really how long I'd be here. I wished she'd just go away. I didn't like being distracted from my surveillance. She moved over to Marjorie Fox and the doppelgänger and I could hear a murmur of conversation, though I couldn't catch the words. It looked as though they were ordering something, and a few minutes later the same waitress came back with two cups of coffee. I was glad I hadn't ordered anything myself because I now saw you had to pay for the drinks. It sounds rather stupid but the way the waitress had asked me I hadn't been sure if the hotel just provided them if you were waiting in the lounge. Anyway I knew better now.

The doppelgänger and Marjorie Fox were obviously discussing the papers, which seemed to be spread out in front of them on the table.

Then I had a brilliant idea! I'd already told the waitress I was waiting for my parents, so why shouldn't I stroll over to the front entrance and peer through the door as though I expected them to appear at any moment? I'd look at my watch as well, as though it might be later than the time we'd agreed to meet. Rory seemed quite busy at the reception desk now so he'd be unlikely to stop me if I looked convincing enough.

I put the magazine back on the table next to me and got up, strolling over to the doors and glancing at my watch. I didn't look at the doppelgänger or Marjorie Fox on the way. They could check me out first if they wanted to! When I got to the doors I peered outside, pushed them open and stood on the pavement for a few seconds, looking up and down the street. Then I came inside the hotel and looked at my watch again, at the same time taking a good look at Marjorie Fox and the doppelgänger. They'd finished their coffee and she was putting the papers back inside the brown envelope, and neither of them seemed to notice me at all. This meant I didn't manage to see the papers properly, but they looked more like a magazine, for example, rather than actual loose papers. The doppelgänger was saying something about the weekend, in a pretty strong accent, but it didn't sound as if that accent was actually a Dutch one; I knew what that ought to sound like. It sounded more like a German accent, perhaps; very similar to Dutch but not the same. Should I ask him something in Dutch? Then he probably wouldn't understand me, and she might get suspicious. But what could I ask him? And anyway, what good would it do? All he had to do was make some excuse and I'd have lost him for good. Surely it was better to follow him still and just somehow make sure I didn't lose him.

I realised Tabi might have been trying to phone me and that I'd switched my phone off so as not to draw attention to myself. But surely she'd have looked through the front windows of the hotel if she'd got here, or else come in the back way as I had? What could have happened to her? She'd said she was only going to be a couple of minutes late.

As I walked back I was able to sit nearer to them than I'd been before, but I was too late to hear much more as they were both standing up and shaking hands again. Marjorie Fox went out of the hotel and turned to the left as soon as she was outside. I guess she was going to the car park. The doppelgänger looked at his watch and put the envelope hastily in his briefcase. He moved very quickly to the door, glanced to the left in the direction of Marjorie Fox, and practically ran down to the right, towards the city centre. He looked as if he was in an awful hurry, like when I'd seen him arrive.

I shot out of the door after him, switching on my phone at the same time to try to reach Tabi.

'I'm not losing you now, you Cascade creep!' I said fiercely. 'No way!'

14

The most amazing discovery. *Unbelievable.*

The doppelgänger headed straight into town and I've never seen anyone supposed to be old move as quickly as he did. It's not easy following someone when they're in a hurry because you have to be in a hurry too and then people are more likely to notice you. When we reached the market stalls at the bottom of the hill it was difficult not to bump into anyone. I focused on the briefcase as much as anything, swinging to and fro among all the people. The doppelgänger was weaving his way through the crowds and once he'd gone past the stall that sells second-hand books I realised he was on his way to the Forum. I didn't take my eyes off him or his briefcase and I knew I wasn't going to lose him.

The Forum is one of the most impressive buildings in Norwich, I think. Apparently it's on the site of a big library that burnt down, and the Forum was built instead as a millennium building. There's a really good library in it, and also the BBC studios, and a café and restaurant and a shop. Outside the Forum there are often shows and musicians and all kinds of things going on. Most people see it as the centre of Norwich because there's always something happening there. Our foreign students from Phoenix often go there for coffee and say it's a great place to be; they like watching all the people and listening to all the English round them.

There's only one way into the Forum and it's through giant glass doors. 'He must be going to meet someone there,' I decided. The cafe was pretty full but the doppelgänger walked straight past and headed towards an art exhibition. There are art exhibitions in the Forum nearly every week and this time they were giant multi-coloured abstract paintings, hanging from those large display boards that look like miniature walls. The walls were set up in a zigzag pattern stretching across a lot of the inside floor space. I was sure the doppelgänger hadn't seen me and with all these people about I didn't think it mattered if I stayed pretty close on his heels now. I remembered waiting at the airport for Professor van Zanten and how cross Tabi had been because she'd thought I'd missed him. She must have been mind-reading again because my phone buzzed and it was her.

'Where are you, Ninian?' she asked. 'I'm really sorry, I just couldn't get away earlier. There was no escape,' she added a bit more dramatically.

'I'm at the Forum,' I answered. 'Oh, would you believe it, he's gone into the toilets!' Was I going to have to hang around outside toilets again, like at the airport? I didn't fancy that much. There are definitely better places to be.

'That's great; I'm really close. The lunch thing was up by the Theatre Royal,' she said. 'We'll be there in a minute.'

'We?' I asked, studying a large blob of purple with a few wavy yellow lines on it which was part of the art exhibition. I wondered what the point was of painting something like that, unless you're about three and haven't used paint before, that is. There was a title and price on a label next to it, fixed to the display board. It said 'Fields of the sun' and was for sale for £150. Someone called Amy White had painted it.

'Miles is with me,' Tabi said. 'He's back from Colin's.' Her voice sounded as though she was huffing and puffing, as it does through the phone if you're walking along while you're talking. That sounded good as with three of us we'd be well up to focusing on the case.

However, as she was talking I was thinking. Something was a bit odd. The doppelgänger could have visited a toilet at the hotel. I didn't think he'd had to nip into the Forum one suddenly, as you have to if you've eaten something odd that disagrees with you violently. He'd already been in a hurry, even before he'd met up with Marjorie Fox. And he had headed straight here just now.

My phone went again. 'We can see you, Ninian,' said Tabi, and tapped me on the shoulder as soon as she'd said it. It made me jump as I have to admit that with all the people around I hadn't seen her coming up. She'd got her striped bag over her shoulder again and Miles was with her. 'Hi, Ninian,' he said, smiling up at me. 'Thanks for the message. I understood the French.'

'Look, I don't like this,' I said. 'There's something odd. He's been in there for a few minutes now. I'm going in.' I didn't know if Tabi had brought Miles up to date about what was going on, but I thought it was time to check things out. It hadn't occurred to me before but suppose the doppelgänger was actually meeting someone in the toilets? I knew it was highly unlikely as only really weird people would surely agree to meet there, but it would be stupid not to check, particularly after the business at the airport when the professor had been bundled into a wheelchair by the stewardess.

Before I could do so, however, Miles gave me a nudge and grabbed Tabi by the arm.

'I don't believe it!' he said. ' It's Thor!' He moved behind me so as not to be spotted.

There was a man coming out of the men's toilets. He was quite tall and had fairish hair, and he was stooping slightly. I was so preoccupied thinking about the doppelgänger that I had to think for a second who Miles meant by Thor. Of course, it was the student from Phoenix that we'd been intending to follow before we'd had

Dad's message. Miles and his friend Colin had followed him for a while yesterday.

'This is exactly where I lost him before,' continued Miles. 'How weird. I've found him again... in just the same place...' I knew what he meant. It was as if a story had stopped suddenly halfway through and then continued again; as if someone had pressed the 'pause' button on a CD player and then let it go.

However that wasn't as incredible as it might have been, because suddenly everything began to fall into place in my head. It was almost as if I'd heard a great crash of thunder overhead and seen several flashes of lightning. I'd been following the doppelgänger's briefcase like a hawk. I'd been wondering all the time what was inside it. By now I could have recognised that briefcase almost anywhere. The very same briefcase was in Thor Rasmussen's hand. And Thor Rasmussen's head was exactly the same shape as that of the doppelgänger, because... they were one and the same person! Of course I knew what was in the briefcase – a wig, and a beard, and a jacket! And, of course, an envelope.

'You're brilliant, Miles!' I exclaimed, giving him a hug.

15

Visiting the Broads with Maurice Vaughan Travel

What good cover! It wouldn't occur to anyone that this ordinary student from Denmark, in Norwich for an English language course, was actually over here as part of a Cascade plan involving kidnapping and theft. And if he stayed for an extra couple of days after stealing whatever he'd got from Marjorie Fox, to look extra convincing, there would be nothing at all to link him to Professor van Zanten! Why should the police ever connect the two? Hundreds of foreign students come to Norwich every week for language courses. If we hadn't found out who he really was no-one would ever have caught him out. I felt really proud that we were Ignis Investigators! And even though Dad knew something was going on in connection with Professor van Zanten he didn't know about Thor at all! He was going to be extremely impressed!

Suddenly I remembered the trip to the Broads that Mum had mentioned that morning. The students must be about to set off from Phoenix in their coach. That was why the doppelgänger, or rather Thor, was in such a hurry. After all, he was pretending to be a perfectly ordinary student from Denmark so he'd be going on the trip too. He'd been really hard pushed to get from his meeting at the Norfolk Way Hotel with Marjorie Fox to the Phoenix Language School and still be able to have time to change out of his wig and everything on the way. No wonder he'd looked really stressed. And now I realised that when I'd heard him speak to Marjorie Fox the reason that his accent hadn't sounded quite like a Dutch one was simply because it had been a Danish one instead.

I looked at my watch.

'Quick!' I said to Tabi and Miles. 'The students are off to the Broads at any moment. He'll be going with them. Come on!' Thor had already gone down the steps outside the Forum and turned left towards St Giles. Phoenix was only a couple of streets further.

'But what do we do? He'll probably take off somewhere now he's got the envelope – and whatever's in it,' said Tabi.

'Can't we just grab the briefcase and run off?' said Miles. 'I mean, we'll never get it otherwise.' He's pretty practical sometimes and I saw his point. If we didn't do something quickly we'd lose Thor for ever.

We were incredibly lucky really, because when we rounded the corner there wasn't a coach outside Phoenix yet, just a group of students waiting either on the pavement outside or on the steps. This was going to give us a few extra minutes to decide what to do, before Thor went to Wroxham, or Hickling, or whichever part of the Broads they were all going off to. Usually they start at Wroxham and get one of the big tour boats there. Mum came out of the building and stood in the doorway as Thor went in, and they exchanged a few words. We were too far away to hear what they were saying but it looked as though Mum was checking everyone off on a list. She was holding one of those flat clipboards like a piece of cardboard, and had a pen in her hand. The pen was probably one of our own ones, which are blue and have 'Phoenix Language School Norwich' printed along the side.

'As long as he gets on the coach we're OK,' said Tabi. Thor was going up the steps and into the building. 'And he must be going on the trip or he wouldn't have hurried so much, would he?' Mum caught sight of us and waved. She was still checking people off on

75

her list. We didn't go up to her but crossed over and stood near the group of students. A few other people were passing on the pavement and we stood to one side to let them pass.

'Accessories!' said Tabi suddenly.

'What are you on about?' I asked. I was desperately trying to come up with a brilliant scheme and couldn't imagine why she needed to talk about umbrellas and scarves and things at this crucial moment. I know she's into stuff like that but what had all that got to do with Thor?

'He'll never take the briefcase on the coach,' she said. 'I mean, people don't, do they? Not when they're going on a boat looking at water birds and reeds and coastal areas and things. It would look stupid – and very odd. People would notice, wouldn't they?' Of course she was right. It would look very strange if Thor spent the whole afternoon clutching a rather formal-looking old-fashioned briefcase. It was one thing in Norwich, when he was going to and from his language course, and people would assume there were things like papers and dictionaries in it, but quite another if he was lugging it round on a boat trip looking at nature. If he was trying to look normal he'd have to leave it behind him this afternoon.

Then we heard the coach coming round the corner behind us and it pulled up outside Phoenix. It wasn't the same company as the one that had been outside the hotel. This was orange and had white letters saying 'Visit the Broads with Maurice Vaughan Travel'. Tabi was proved right, thank goodness, because Thor came down the steps without the briefcase, joining the group of people waiting. The driver of the coach got out and came round to talk to Mum, and then the students began to get in. I couldn't believe our luck, because he had to have left the briefcase inside the building. I realised where he must have left it, too, because whenever students want to leave anything valuable they always ask Sharon at the front desk to look after it. I knew we'd think of a way to lure Sharon away from her desk somehow – and then we'd actually get the chance to have a look inside that envelope!

16

Happy Tunes for Little Hands *(piano book for beginners)*

Once the coach had left we went up to the flat and into the kitchen, where I opened a packet of chocolate biscuits and gave Tabi and Miles all the details about Thor's meeting with Marjorie Fox. I told them how I'd gone outside the hotel pretending to look for someone, too, so as to get a better look at what they'd been doing. I'd been right about Miles knowing what Tabi and I had been doing for the last few days, because Tabi had brought him pretty much up to date with everything. It was just as well; we'd never have worked out this puzzle if Miles hadn't been there to spot Thor in the Forum. Apparently Miles' friend Colin hadn't thought much of spending his time following people so Miles hadn't been tempted to reveal anything about Ignis to him.

'Wouldn't it be funny,' said Miles thoughtfully, 'if he wasn't really Thor either. I mean, he could be a different Cascade person, making up a new name to come to England in the first place.' Tabi and I laughed.

'So he wouldn't be "Doppy" at all,' said Tabi. 'He'd be... what's the German for "triple", Ninian?'

'Tripel,' I said quickly. 'He'd be a "tripelgänger"!' That was a thought. It could be a new word in dictionaries! For a moment I imagined looking into a shop window and seeing a reflection of two more of myself standing behind me. I knew I'd be completely freaked! Probably permanently!

'Anyway,' I said, 'We need that envelope now. After all it belongs to Professor van Zanten really.'

'We can easily get Sharon away from her desk, can't we?' said Tabi. 'We can pretend there's something wrong in a classroom or something. Then she'll have to go and have a look.'

'And we can help ourselves to the envelope while she's gone,' said Miles. 'It'll only take a minute.'

Then I had the most fantastic idea, and it was so brilliant that I jumped up and leapt around the kitchen for a few seconds.

'What on earth is it, Ninian?' Tabi asked. 'Have you gone stark raving mad?'

'No, not at all,' I said. 'But eureka, eureka! I've just thought of the most perfect nasty thing for us to do!' I liked saying 'eureka'. I'd remembered it when I was leaping round the kitchen, and it's Greek for 'I have found'. It's quite a famous word because a guy called Archimedes in Ancient Greece said it when he thought up some plan or other. I think it was something to do with gold in a crown. Anyway it sounds good saying it when you have an incredible idea.

'Nasty?' said Miles. 'Why nasty?'

'Listen,' I said. 'We're going to get that envelope, right? But if he comes back at the end of the afternoon and looks in his briefcase for anything he'll see straight away it's gone, won't he? And then he'll know the game's up, and... well, warn the others or something.'

'That's true,' said Tabi. 'He'll guess straight away that someone's onto him.'

'This is my plan,' I said, rather importantly. I knew they'd love this. 'I saw what was in that envelope when Marjorie Fox gave it to him, and whatever it actually was it's the same size as a magazine. So what we do is leave the envelope in the briefcase and just take out what's inside. And then we put back something else instead so he can see the envelope's got something in it.

That way he'll never guess anything's happened. At least not straight away,' I added.

'OK, great, let's go and get a magazine and swap it now,' said Miles.

'Ah, but this is the best bit,' I said. 'Just wait here!'

They both looked very surprised as I got up again and went off down the hall to my room. When I came back in I showed them what I'd fetched.

'You know I was supposed to clear up all that stuff in my room?' I said, brandishing something which was the size of a magazine. 'Well, look! This is my old piano book from ages ago. When I thought I wanted to learn and then didn't like it at all. What we do is put this in the envelope instead. It's just the right size. Can you imagine his face when he finds it? I mean, can you?'

'Oh, that is awesome!' laughed Tabi. 'Wow, Ninian, great! "Happy Tunes for Little Hands",' she read, looking at the title. 'I would love to be there to see his face! Specially if there are other Cascade people there too, all waiting to get their hands on the real papers!'

'Seriously nasty!' exclaimed Miles, looking really pleased.

'Right,' I said. 'First we've got to be sure that the briefcase really is with Sharon. Then I'll get her away from her desk while you swap the music for the papers. Only you'll have to be quick. I'll never be able to keep her away for long. And the phone might go or something.'

'How are you going to divert her attention?' asked Tabi.

'I'll get her down to one of the basement classrooms, like you suggested,' I said. 'It'll take her a couple of minutes to go down and have a look. Leave it to me. You be ready here to nip downstairs and do the swap as soon as she's gone.' I got out my mobile and switched it on. 'I'll go out the back way,' I said. There's a fire escape down into our garden which I use as ordinary stairs sometimes. 'I'll call you as soon as she's down there. Get ready.'

I took Mum's spare set of keys from the wall and opened the back door, which leads from the kitchen onto the metal fire escape. Tabi and Miles had picked up the piano music and went out of the kitchen, ready to go down to the Phoenix entrance to Sharon's desk as soon as I gave the signal. As long as Sharon didn't realise what we were up to this ought to be successful.

When you go down the fire escape your feet clang on the metal stairs. We don't use it that often as usually we just use the front door, and anyway there's always the side gate if I want to get my bike or anything. When I reached the garden I peered through the narrow windows into the basement classrooms. There was no-one inside so everyone must have gone on the trip to the Broads. At any rate there were no lessons taking place there at all. I looked at the keys in my hand, selecting what might be a suitable one, and jumped down the low brick wall into the little basement area by the classrooms, because there is a fire door there; if everyone ever had to get out of the basement in a hurry they could get up into our garden and escape that way. It's just as well because there's no door from the basement onto the street at the front of the building. My idea was to go into one of the classrooms and start making quite a noise, so that Sharon would hear it and go down to find out what was happening. She knew Mum expected me to tidy the classrooms sometimes so wouldn't be that surprised once she found it was only me. She wouldn't expect me to go through the garden to get there but that didn't really matter.

I unlocked the door, pulled it open, and went through into the smaller classroom because it's nearer the stairs so Sharon would be more likely to hear me. I turned one of the long tables over rather violently so it crashed onto the floor, and then knocked a couple of chairs over too. Then I started dragging the upside-down table along towards the window, so it would make scraping noises.

Surely she'd hear all this? And I was right, because in hardly any time at all I heard her calling down the stairs,

'Is everything alright down there? Can I help?' I deliberately didn't answer so that she'd have to come down to see, and the plan worked. I could hear her coming so quickly rang Tabi. 'Go go go!' I said into the phone.

It didn't take long to convince Sharon that I'd knocked a table over by mistake. She must have thought I was pretty stupid, though. She didn't ask why I hadn't gone down the proper stairs to get in. To keep her talking and give the others more time to change the papers I asked her when the Broads trip was going to be back.

'Oh, they won't be back for at least three hours,' she said. 'But make sure you leave this classroom looking neat, Ninian. Do try to be more careful. That was an awful noise. I'd rather you didn't hang around down here, either.' Hang around! Little did she know. And anyway, I do live in the building.

'Could you just help me lift this table back up, please, Sharon?' I asked really politely. I could see she'd decided she had better things to do upstairs but she did help me turn the table and set it back where it had been.

'Thank you, Sharon,' I said meekly.

As soon as she'd gone out of the classroom to make her way upstairs again I went back out into the garden. I wasn't going to put the chairs straight now; I could do that later today.

It would be far more interesting to find out what was in the brown envelope!

17

Xibu ofyu? *(code message)*

Tabi and Miles had acted very fast; they told me that they'd been able to get upstairs completely out of sight before Sharon came up the stairs again. They'd heard the murmur of conversation in the basement while I'd been talking to her. The briefcase had been under the counter, waiting for Thor's return. It had been easy for them to open the briefcase, take the papers out of the envelope and substitute the music for them.

'We put the envelope back exactly where it had been,' said Tabi. 'Next to the wig, and on the other side of his English book. And the opening of the envelope is the same way round too.'

'He'll never notice,' said Miles. 'It all looks just the same. But the wig looks weird without a head in it.'

I could imagine what he'd seen. The wig probably looked like some kind of animal, curled up. And I suppose you could roll up a false beard.

As Mum had gone on the Broads trip too we knew we wouldn't be disturbed for a while. Sharon never comes up to the flat. Tabi had put the papers on the kitchen table and we gathered round to look at them. Although at first I'd thought they were bound or stapled together, like a magazine, there was actually a large piece of paper folded round several loose papers. The large paper was like a cardboard file, keeping the smaller papers together. Some of the papers were in Dutch and some were in English, and to be honest they didn't look very interesting at all. I felt really disappointed and I guessed that the others were too.

'Is that all?' said Miles, frowning. 'What's so special about these?'

'I don't know,' I said, looking through them. There were a couple of letters, one from someone in Leiden called Heffinck and one going on about someone called Julian in Norwich, and the Dutch was really old-fashioned. The letters had obviously been written a long time ago. It was something to do with paintings but there weren't any pictures with the papers. And there was a newspaper article from an English paper dated 1984 about a painting which had been found in a building in Elm Hill, Norwich. That didn't surprise me because the buildings in Elm Hill are really old and some of them are art galleries. Maybe someone had bought a painting there which had turned out to be worth a lot of money. Or perhaps a really special work of art had been found in someone's attic. That does happen sometimes. Whatever the case, I didn't feel like studying the papers all afternoon.

'I don't get it,' said Tabi. 'These papers don't look valuable at all. But for some reason Zanto needs them and they must be worth a lot of money or Cascade wouldn't steal them, would they?'

'Well, the main thing is we've got them now,' I said. 'So what we really ought to do is give them back to the professor. Only we can't because Cascade have still got him.'

'Yes,' said Tabi. 'Do you think they will just let him go now?'

'I don't see why not,' I said. 'They think they've got what they want. But how long is Thor going to be hanging around? Maybe he's got to give the papers to someone else.'

'Perhaps that's why he's left them here,' said Tabi. 'He may have arranged to have them collected today, from Phoenix I mean.'

We hadn't thought of that. Thor might have told Sharon that the briefcase was going to be fetched this afternoon and asked her to give it to whoever asked for it. And that wasn't really something we could question Sharon about. On the other hand Thor would hardly want to draw Sharon's attention to the case. She might look inside and find the wig!

How many people were involved in this? Perhaps the stewardess who had kidnapped the professor would be collecting the papers. Although I was really pleased we'd got them I couldn't see what we ought to do next. How could we find out how the professor was? Was he going to be all right? And as I was wondering all this there was suddenly a noise in the hall. Someone was breaking into the flat! For a moment I almost panicked, thinking that somehow Cascade must have found out that we'd got the papers and was coming after us to get them back. Tabi and Miles froze too. They must have been thinking the same thing. But then I heard a familiar step and the sound of a suitcase being put down.

'Dad!' I cried, rushing over to him.

18

Dénouement *(French)*
The unravelling of a story, the outcome of events

After that there was a lot of talking. We were keen to explain what had happened since Professor van Zanten had arrived at Norwich airport. Dad wanted us to describe all the people carefully and he was pleased we'd got several photos to show him on our mobiles. As soon as I'd started to tell him about Kingfisher Cabins he'd written a few notes on the back of a piece of paper and had then gone to make some phone calls from the study. Then he'd come back to hear the rest of our story. He laughed really hard when he heard about us substituting the piano music for the Heffinck papers.

'What about the professor, Dad?' I asked when we'd finished and shown him the papers which were still lying on the kitchen table. 'I mean, is he really going to be all right? I felt awful leaving him there but I just couldn't see what I could do.'

Dad looked a little grim but he said, 'No, I think he'll be fine. That's what one of my phone calls was about. If I'm right he's being picked up now, along with your stewardess. It's you I'm more concerned about. That could have got very nasty if you'd been discovered.'

He looked at his watch.

'Well, Ninian, your mother won't be back yet, and I was hoping to surprise her this afternoon.'

'I thought you weren't coming till the end of the week, Uncle Leon,' said Tabi.

'No, I wasn't,' said Dad. 'But one of my meetings in China was cancelled, and I decided not to stop off in Singapore.'

'So who are these Cascade people?' asked Miles. 'Why are the papers so important?'

'Yes, now it's your turn, Dad,' I said. 'We've told you what we've been doing since we got your message. What is it all about?'

Dad leant back in his chair.

'Let's just say that I heard from a friend that certain people had their eye on Professor van Zanten. He's a well-known authority on sixteenth century Dutch painting and he's come to Norwich for a conference at the university which starts next week. He'll be giving some lectures there. I had no idea that he'd be captured as soon as he arrived. And it's not kidnapping really, by the way, because no-one's asking for ransom money. While he's over here he'll be studying a couple of paintings which have turned up which may or may not be worth a great deal of money. We understood that he was going to be persuaded to say that they aren't by the artist they might be by.'

'The artist they might be by?' interrupted Tabi. 'But what if they aren't?'

'It's almost certain that the paintings he'll be shown are worth thousands of pounds – even millions,' said Dad. 'But as he's the expert, if he says they are worthless, Cascade will be able to buy them at auction for practically nothing. And then later...'

'They will sell them as the real thing,' I completed.

'The art world is full of criminals,' said Dad.

'So how much are these papers worth?' asked Miles, indicating the Heffinck papers that he and Tabi had removed from the briefcase.

'Don't be too disappointed,' said Dad. 'I'm really impressed with what you've been doing and I don't blame you for thinking that those were what Cascade wanted. In fact they aren't important, just something that that woman – what's her name again?'

'Marjorie Fox,' I put in.

'Yes, that Marjorie Fox needed to give the professor. And your doppelgänger must have wondered what on earth they were. His work is really supposed to start next week at the conference.'

'So why didn't they wait till next week to kidnap, I mean capture, the professor?' I asked.

'As you say, it's better cover,' Dad replied. 'You're absolutely right about Thor Rasmussen's cover as a student, and by taking the professor as soon as he arrived no-one would get a chance to discover what he really looked like. Professor van Zanten doesn't get about much nowadays, apparently. I don't think he's been in England for a very long time.'

Then the telephone went in the study, and Dad went off to answer it. When he came back he was looking really pleased.

'The professor's safe,' he said. 'And certain people are extremely grateful to you, because if it hadn't been for you they wouldn't have been able to find him.'

As Dad said that I asked myself not for the first time why he had asked Ignis to carry out surveillance on the professor. Was it really true that no-one had been expecting anything to happen until the conference started? Or had Dad been using us because no-one would expect people our age to be on the case? I decided that there was more to what Dad had been telling us than he was giving away.

'What about the stewardess?' I asked, remembering how scary her voice had sounded when she'd arrived at the cabin in the woods.

'Oh, she's quite well-known,' Dad answered. 'Although her bark is worse than her bite. She'll be back in prison where she belongs before you can say "doppelgänger"!'

We all laughed. Dad looked at his watch. 'That coach will be back any minute,' he said. 'I need you out of the way for a little while. But I promise your Thor won't get away. And I know you want to see his face when he finds the music. I'll see what I can do.' That sounded encouraging.

'You're sure?' asked Miles.

'Oh, yes,' said Dad, smiling again. 'I've had an idea.'

We left the Heffinck papers with Dad and went to chill out at Tabi and Miles' for a little while. I knew Dad would be on the phone picking up all the loose ends he said he needed to sort to make sure that Thor and the stewardess were dealt with properly. And Mum would be surprised to find Dad there when she got home!

'What about James Conrad?' asked Tabi suddenly. 'Uncle Leon didn't ask much about him, did he? Where do you think he disappeared to after meeting the professor at the airport? We haven't seen him anywhere since.'

'No,' I said thoughtfully. 'Do you think he went off on a plane somewhere? I wonder what Dad thinks about that?' We had talked so much through with Dad, but we hadn't got any more details out of him about James Conrad.

'Ninian, what does Uncle Leon really do?' asked Miles suddenly. 'I mean, how come he knows all about art thieves, and who was he phoning?'

'I don't really know,' I said. 'At least, I'm not exactly sure,' I added. I didn't want to sound completely ignorant about what Dad got up to but I was now absolutely convinced that when he went abroad it wasn't just to recruit students. This all proved it!

Epilogue – *the concluding section of a book*

It was nearly supper time when Dad phoned me on my mobile.

'Ignis Investigators?' he said, and his voice was very cheerful indeed. 'Get home quickly, will you, Ninian? And bring Tabi and Miles. We're going to the airport.'

We shot round to Phoenix and there was a taxi waiting outside. I suddenly had a strange feeling and looked at the driver, but it wasn't the one I'd asked to follow the Renault with the professor inside. That might have been a bit embarrassing.

'We're doing this in style,' Dad explained. 'I know you want to be in at the kill.'

I thought Dad looked pretty tired, but he sounded awfully pleased. Mum waved us off from the steps, so Dad must have been telling her all about everything. She looked relaxed too so I decided we weren't going to be told off about following students. Though I remembered I hadn't finished tidying up that basement classroom yet.

I assumed we'd be meeting someone at the airport, though I didn't know who. Dad had been silent nearly all the way there.

'Follow me,' he said when we pulled up outside the entrance doors. 'We've been doing some message interception and sending a few of our own, and your doppelgänger thinks he's meeting a friend off the Amsterdam flight.'

'You haven't arrested him, then?' asked Miles.

Dad turned to him.

'You have to be able to prove things before you arrest someone,' he said. 'That's why this has been set up.'

He led the way round towards the arrivals lounge. This was where Tabi and I had stood waiting for the professor. But this time Dad opened a grey door into an office. There was a tall young man in uniform there who got up and shook hands as we entered.

'So these are the detectives,' said the man, looking us over. He sounded friendly but I wished Dad had explained what was going to happen. Why were we here?

'Good evening, David,' said Dad. 'Yes. We thought we'd come and watch your televisions.'

On one wall of the room we saw that there were several screens. On the screens were people walking round the airport building, sitting at the café and checking in suitcases. It was CCTV! Dad pointed to one of the screens.

'Here he comes now,' he said.

As we watched, Thor Rasmussen walked up to someone in the arrivals lounge. He had the briefcase with him. When the other man turned round we could see who it was. The picture on the screen was really clear.

'It's Connie!' exclaimed Tabi. 'He's back!'

On the screen we saw Thor and James Conrad shake hands, and as soon as they had, three security guards appeared as if from nowhere.

'Are they being arrested?' asked Miles.

'Oh, yes,' said the man called David. 'I understand you want to be there for the interview?'

He pointed through a doorway behind his desk. I'd thought it was just a cupboard or something but it was a small room and one wall was in fact a large window with rather odd-looking glass in it. If you looked through the window you could see a table and chairs. And as we peered through, Thor was led into the room by a security guard. They sat down at the table and didn't look up. The window we were looking through must have been one of those one-way mirrors. And there must have been a microphone too, because the security guard began to speak. He glanced briefly up in our direction, so perhaps he knew we were there.

'Put your briefcase on the desk, please, and open it,' he said to Thor.

'Now for it!' whispered Miles, trembling a little with excitement. The three of us leaned forward for a perfect view.

Thor put the briefcase on the desk. There was nothing else he could do. He opened it, and the guard took out all the things one by one.

'The wig!' whispered Tabi, giggling.

'And the beard!' added Miles, nudging me.

'Open the envelope, please,' said the guard.

So then it happened. Thor didn't look very pleased as he opened the flap. He pulled out the music book.

I don't think I've ever seen anyone look so surprised! Shocked, in fact! His jaw really did drop several centimetres! Tabi, Miles and I burst out laughing.

'Right,' said Dad. 'I'm afraid we have to leave the rest to the authorities to wind this up. We're off home. Thanks for this, David.'

'No problem, Leon,' he answered. 'I won't say "any time", but you're welcome.'

And that was it really. Dad told us in the taxi home that James Conrad was actually the most Cascade person of all in this case. He'd been involved in a great many art thefts and scams and travelled on several passports, all in different names. So he was more important in the Cascade world than the stewardess or the doppelgänger.

'How do you feel about things, Ignis Investigators?' asked Dad as the taxi drew up outside Phoenix. 'Up for another case some time?'

'Definitely,' I said, looking at the others. 'And it's only the beginning of the Easter holidays!'

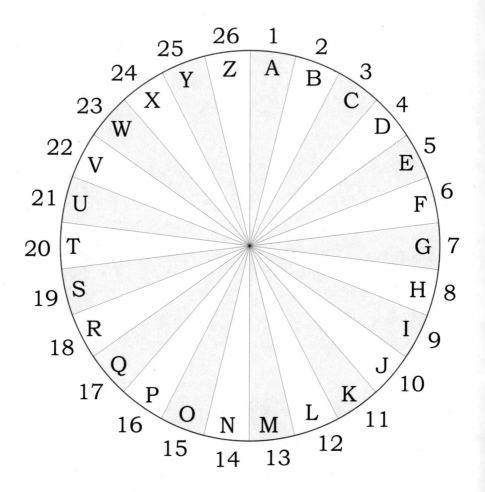